THE SECRETS OF
Eastcliff-by-the-Sea

The Story of ANNALIESE EASTERLING & THROCKMORTON,

Her Simply Remarkable Sock Monkey

EILEEN BEHA

illustrated by
Sarah Jane Wright

Beach Lane Books

New York London Toronto Sydney New Delhi

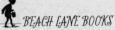 BEACH LANE BOOKS

An imprint of Simon & Schuster Children's Publishing Division
1230 Avenue of the Americas, New York, New York 10020
This book is a work of fiction. Any references to historical events,
real people, or real places are used fictitiously. Other names, characters, places,
and events are products of the author's imagination, and any resemblance
to actual events or places or persons, living or dead, is entirely coincidental.
Text copyright © 2014 by Eileen Beha
Cover and interior illustrations by Sarah Jane Wright
All rights reserved, including the right of reproduction
in whole or in part in any form.
Beach Lane Books is a trademark of Simon & Schuster, Inc.
For information about special discounts for bulk purchases, please contact Simon
& Schuster Special Sales at 1-866-506-1949 or business@simonandschuster.com.
The Simon & Schuster Speakers Bureau can bring authors to your live event. For
more information or to book an event, contact the Simon & Schuster Speakers
Bureau at 1-866-248-3049 or visit our website at www.simonspeakers.com.
Also available in a hardcover edition.
Book design by Lauren Rille
The text for this book is set in Bell.
Manufactured in the United States of America
0917 OFF
First paperback edition September 2015
10 9 8 7 6 5 4 3
The Library of Congress has cataloged the hardcover edition as follows:
Beha, Eileen.
The Secrets of Eastcliff-by-the-Sea : the story of Annaliese Easterling &
Throckmorton, her simply remarkable sock monkey / by Eileen Beha ;
illustrated by Sarah Jane Wright.—First edition.
p. cm.
Summary: An abandoned sock monkey's adventurous quest to reunite his owner
with the one person she most longs to know.
ISBN 978-1-4424-9840-2 (hardcover)
ISBN 978-1-4424-9842-6 (eBook)
[1. Toys—Fiction. 2. Mothers—Fiction. 3. Separation (Psychology)—Fiction.]
I. Sarah Jane Wright, illustrator. II. Title.
PZ7.B3882191Th 2014
[Fic]—dc23
2013044880
ISBN 978-1-4424-9841-9 (pbk)

For Jane Resh Thomas,
my writing mentor and friend,
who loved this story from the beginning

Once, in a fine house on a high cliff above a frozen sea, Throckmorton S. Monkey heard the frenzied barks of the family dogs announcing the approach of a stranger.

Throckmorton, a hand-sewn sock monkey, was suspended at the time in a fishy-smelling net strung high above Annaliese Easterling's frosting pink four-poster bed.

Dozens of stuffed animals were stored in the crowded net.

Pressed against Throckmorton's embroidered nose was the fuzzy tail of a stuffed rabbit. A penguin's beak poked his black button eye. An elephant's ear, spotted with jam, stuck to his bright red rump.

Throckmorton was miserable.

Many months earlier, a lazy maid named Madge— a fisherman's daughter—had tossed him into the odoriferous net, and Annaliese hadn't ever bothered to fish him out.

The maid said that she was sick and tired of dusting dolls that Annaliese never played with and pressing dresses she rarely wore. Mostly, Madge was sick and tired of scooping up stuffed toys off of the nine-year-old girl's messy bedroom floor.

Rats, rats, double-rats!

Whatever had Throckmorton done to deserve such a cruel fate?

Why, he'd done everything that a red-heeled sock monkey was supposed to do. He'd been all that a red-heeled sock monkey was expected to be:

Loving.

Loyal.

A very good listener.

And he'd never—not even once!—stopped smiling.

Nonetheless, here he was . . . netted like a common crab.

Life, he lamented anew, was so unfair.

Suddenly the doorbell rang.

Who could it be? he wondered.

Eastcliff-by-the-Sea was far, far away from it all. The manor house was old and not nearly as fine as it used to be. Visitors of any kind were rare.

Now Donald and Bailey had stopped barking, and from somewhere in the house, Annaliese was shouting, "Evan! Teddy! Come here! Come quick!"

Neither brother answered her call.

Trippety-trip, trippety-trip . . . the heels of her shoes clicked as she scurried up the servants' staircase to the second floor.

Thrickety-thrump, thrickety-thrump . . . the soles

of her shoes drummed as she scuttled through the manor's shadowy halls.

"Miss Pine! Miss Pine! Come here! Come quick!"

Throckmorton was dying to know what the excitement was all about. If only he had bones and muscles, he thought wistfully, he'd dive into the frothy sea of pillows on Annaliese's bed below and dash after her.

If only he weren't so miserable . . .

Forgotten, abandoned, and unable to break free.

If truth be told, Annaliese Easterling had once loved Throckmorton dearly. He'd been hugged and snuggled, bedded and cuddled. She'd tickled his ears and twirled his soft body by the tail. Daily they'd taken tea at the tiny lace-covered table in the corner of her room.

To his credit, Throckmorton had tried to accept his abandonment without bitterness. After all, he told himself, Annaliese was part of a very large—not to mention very wealthy—family. She could play with a doll or stuffed toy for only so long before some rich but distant relative sent her a new one.

Alas, doing time in the net had taught Throckmorton a cruel lesson. Now he understood that his love and loyalty, listening and never-ending smile weren't quite good enough. And that someday, he'd need to do something so remarkable that Annaliese would never forget about him again.

Buoyed by his resolve to achieve the impossible, the burden of self-pity lightened a little. He barely heard the bedroom door swish open.

"I think he's in there!" Annaliese cried breathlessly.

"Up in that smelly old net?" asked Miss Pine, the new nanny, whose voice Throckmorton recognized.

"I think so," Annaliese answered. "I mean, I hope so."

"Oh my," the nanny sighed.

Miss Pine, who was very, very tall, unhooked the bulging net. The jumble of stuffed toys tumbled out and Throckmorton landed faceup on a furry rug—free at last!

Annaliese dropped to her knees. She brushed a plush pony's tail out of his eyes and pulled him into a hug. "Oh, Throckmorton," she murmured, "I've missed you so."

Now, Throckmorton knew that his broad red smile was telling Annaliese that he'd missed her, too. However, a tad bit of resentment still lingered inside his stuffing.

"Guess what?" his fickle little mistress chirped.

She jiggled an envelope—square, stamped, and scarlet red—in front of his nose.

"A letter came for you in the mail. Special delivery! Didn't it, Miss Pine?"

"It did indeed."

Since when does a sock monkey get a letter in the mail? Throckmorton's spirits soared.

How perfectly intriguing. . . .

The address that Annaliese read aloud was engraved in a glorious golden script:

Mr. Throckmorton S. Monkey

Eastcliff-by-the-Sea

Bay Fortune, Maine

A perplexed look crossed Miss Pine's face. "What does the *S* stand for?"

Annaliese rolled her eyes. "Sock."

The nanny laughed.

"And what's that?" Miss Pine pointed at a small yellow duck pinned on Throckmorton's chest.

"A diaper pin," Annaliese answered, stroking the little duck's back. "He's had it for as long as I can remember."

"And who . . ." Miss Pine paused.

Throckmorton knew who had stuck the diaper pin to his chest: Olivia, Annaliese's mother, who disappeared when Annaliese was a baby.

Annaliese quickly turned her attention back to the scarlet envelope. "I'll open it, Throckmorton, if it's all right with you. . . ."

"Not so fast," Miss Pine cautioned. "We'd better wait until Judge Easterling gets home from the courthouse. Then we'll open all the sock monkeys' letters at the same time."

All the sock monkeys' letters?

Throckmorton could hardly believe his ears (which were pretzel-shaped, and in his opinion, extremely unbecoming).

"But where are the other sock monkeys?" Annaliese asked.

"Your father never said a thing about having sock monkeys when he hired me," Miss Pine replied. "Children, yes. Sock monkeys, no. And certainly not sock monkeys who get mail."

"Please, Miss Pine? Please may I take just one itty-bitty peek at Throckmorton's letter?"

"No, Miss Easterling, you may not."

"Well then, may I invite Mr. Throckmorton S. Monkey to dinner this evening?"

"But of course."

Invited to dinner? *Huzzah!*

"And a place for you, too, Miss Pine," Annaliese pleaded.

"Oh no, I don't think your father . . . ," the nanny protested.

"But I insist."

"Well, perhaps just this once. . . ."

Egad!

Miss Pine accepted Annaliese's invitation! Didn't the young woman know her place?

Judge Easterling would never allow a nanny to dine with the family, would he?

"Then it's settled," said Annaliese smugly. "Did Mrs. Wiggins tell you what we're having?"

"Lobster bisque, popovers, and banana cream pie."

"How does that sound, Throckmorton?"

He imagined the enticing aroma of maple butter melting on hot popovers.

It sounds wonderful, he thought.

Simply wonderful.

That afternoon, outside Eastcliff's crumbling stone and timber walls, ancient pine trees blackened in the waning light. The winds weakened and snowflakes began to fall, like secrets from a charcoal sky.

Inside the manor's cavernous dining room, Annaliese placed Throckmorton in an ornately carved high chair used by generations of Easterling children. She set his tray with miniature pieces of fine English bone china and a tiny, slightly tarnished silver spoon.

Throckmorton felt like royalty.

Annaliese sat on his left. Evan and Teddy, eleven-year-old twins, sat across from him. The Honorable Judge Ellis Easterling crowned the head of a polished wooden table that was long enough to seat a small army.

A portrait of the family's founder hung on the wall in back of the judge. Throckmorton had often heard the story:

A long, long time ago, Henry Easterling had sailed from Scotland to the northern coast of Maine, where he'd fished the seas, felled the trees,

and skinned the silver foxes of their precious furs, amassing a great fortune. Henry Easterling had built Eastcliff as his summer home, but his descendants lived here year-round.

Miss Pine was seated in a faded brocade dining chair on Throckmorton's right. Annaliese's nanny wore a woodsy fragrance. Her blouse had ruffles, and she'd tied her hair back with a velvet ribbon.

Throckmorton glanced at the judge, wondering if the dreary man would notice her presence.

He didn't.

In fact, the judge was half-finished with his bowl of lobster bisque before his eyes came to rest on Miss Pine's plain face.

"Ah, Miss . . ."

"Miss Pine, sir. Laurel Pine."

"Father," said Teddy, noticeably chagrined. "You hired Miss Pine just last week."

"Why, yes. Yes, of course."

After that exchange, much was eaten but little was said. The judge's gloom was contagious. Throckmorton thought that the meal would never end.

Finally—finally!—Judge Easterling scraped the last bit of whipped cream off his dessert plate.

"Children, Miss Pine, you may be excused."

Annaliese's dimples deepened in her cheeks. "Wait! I have a surprise," she announced.

Miss Pine reached into her skirt pocket. She leaned across the high chair and slipped four red envelopes into Annaliese's hand.

Pressing her lips together with delight, Annaliese delivered the day's mysterious mail to her father. She peeked over his shoulder, rubbing her arms and shivering with excitement.

The judge nodded toward the high-back upholstered chair she'd vacated. "Be a good girl now, Annaliese . . ."

Throckmorton felt a tightness seize his throat. Those four words—*be a good girl*—often seemed like the only words the judge ever spoke to his daughter.

After Annaliese took her seat, Judge Easterling drew a pair of wire-rimmed glasses out of his vest pocket. Scowling, he shuffled through the envelopes.

"What in the world . . . ?"

Then, in a voice best suited for the sentencing of dangerous criminals, he read: "Throckmorton S. Monkey; Captain Eugene S. Monkey; Sir Rudyard S. Monkey; Miss Beatrice S. Monkey."

"Huh?" Evan blurted—the first sound that Annaliese's brother had spoken since dinner began.

The judge's salt-and-pepper mustache twitched. "I demand to know what this is all about."

"The letters came today," Annaliese explained. "A man in a uniform brought them right up to our door. But Miss Pine wouldn't let me open them. Not even Throckmorton's."

The judge plucked an envelope out of the short stack on the table in front of him. Right before he broke the seal, he cast suspicious eyes in Throckmorton's direction. "If you don't mind . . ."

Of course Throckmorton didn't mind! He

couldn't wait to see what was inside.

"It looks like a valentine!" Annaliese exclaimed.

"Who's it from?" asked Teddy.

"Your great-grandmama," the judge answered with a touch of irritation in his voice. "My grandmother on my father's side," he clarified for Miss Pine's benefit.

"She's got oodles of money," Teddy gloated.

Annaliese's palms made rapid taps on the tops of her legs. "Read it," she urged.

Judge Easterling cleared his throat and recited the words precisely as printed on the heart-shaped card:

Mrs. Ethel Constance Easterling
Requests the pleasure of you and your keeper's company
At a party in honor of her ninetieth birthday
Saturday, February 14th
Six o'clock in the evening

♥

The Ballroom
Eastcliff-by-the-Sea

RSVP

The judge snorted. "A party? For sock monkeys?"

For joy, for joy! Throckmorton cheered to himself. A party for sock monkeys!

"On Valentine's Day? That's less than a month away," groused the judge. "Why, there hasn't been a party in the ballroom since . . ."

In his mind, Throckmorton completed the judge's sentence: *since Olivia left . . .*

Not only no parties . . . no music either.

No dancing.

And definitely—most definitely—no joy.

Throckmorton remembered how Olivia's fingers once flew across harp strings like fairies in flight. And how, when her vagabond friends brought their fiddles, flutes, tin whistles, and drums to the Eastcliff ballroom, the crotchety old manor house sprang to life.

"The least my own grandmother could've done," the judge grumbled, "is *asked* to use our ballroom before . . ."

"*Our* ballroom?" Evan chided, rubbing salt in his father's old wound. "I thought you said that Great-Grandmama still owns Eastcliff, even if she does allow us to live here."

"She's up to something. . . ."

A sock monkey birthday ball, that's what she's up to! Throckmorton was so happy, he feared his seams might split.

After taking a draught of tea, the judge stroked his five-o'clock shadow, as if deep in thought.

Miss Pine broke the uncomfortable silence. "Excuse me, sir, but where did the sock monkeys come from?"

"Whenever a baby is born into the family, Great-Grandmama Easterling makes a sock monkey."

Now, it was common knowledge that Ethel Constance Easterling had spent most of her wild and wealthy life pursuing fickle whims, exotic places, and four husbands. Her adoration of sock monkeys was deemed just one more curious aberration of character.

"I see. . . . ," said Miss Pine.

"We all have one," the judge told her.

"They come with birth certificates," Teddy added.

"I've never seen your sock monkey, Father," said Annaliese. "Where is it?"

The skin above Judge Easterling's white shirt collar reddened. "Um, I guess I don't know where she is."

"She?" Evan sneered. "Yours is a girl?"

"Yes," the judge acknowledged. "Miss Beatrice."

Although he'd never seen Miss Beatrice, Throckmorton felt sorry for the judge's sock monkey. Through firsthand experience, he'd learned how dreadful it felt to be forgotten by your keeper.

"Well, Captain Eugene is mine," Teddy said. "Sir Rudyard belongs to Evan, even if he won't admit it."

"Sir Rudyard. What a stupid name," said Evan. "No wonder I ditched that thing."

Sir Rudyard was hardly stupid, Throckmorton silently protested.

Au contraire . . . Sir Rudyard S. Monkey was the largest, and considered the smartest, in the long line of sock monkeys that Great-Grandmama Easterling had made. Sir Rudyard was also impeccably dressed: a white shirt and bow tie; suspenders and herringbone slacks; and a tiny round gold watch in the pocket of his paisley vest.

Abruptly, Evan pushed his chair away from the table. "Anyway, who cares? I'm not going. Teddy and I always play pond hockey on Saturday nights."

"Hold on, Son."

The judge distributed the invitations like a man dealing cards: "Throckmorton, Annaliese; Captain Eugene, Teddy; Sir Rudyard, Evan; and Miss Beatrice, me."

"Great," Evan groaned.

"Now, no more skating or games of any sort until the missing monkeys are found."

Evan punched the air. "Aw, Father, that's not fair."

"Life," the judge declared, "is never fair."

"And perhaps it's a good thing for most of us that life is not fair," piped Miss Pine.

Throckmorton just about tipped over.

No nanny talked back to Judge Easterling.

Ever.

His eyes bore into her. "Would you care to elaborate?"

The corners of Miss Pine's mouth turned up slightly and she met his gaze. "Oh, just something my favorite poet once said . . ."

The judge checked his watch. Grim and eager as he always was to retire to his study, he waved his hand dismissively. "Take care of this business, Miss Pine," he told her, turning on his heel.

"The, um, monkey business?" she asked.

Miss Pine winked at Throckmorton.

"Oh yes, sir. I will, sir. You can count on me, sir."

A few hours later, in front of a massive stone fireplace in Eastcliff's two-story library, Annaliese sat cross-legged on a brown bearskin rug. Burning logs of silver birch cast shifting shadows on Annaliese's dejected expression.

Teddy had gone off on his own after dinner to look for the missing sock monkeys. He hadn't asked his little sister to come along. Annaliese and Throckmorton joined Evan's search instead. Down in Eastcliff's dank, dark cellar, Evan deserted them. Annaliese and Throckmorton skedaddled back up to the library.

Miss Pine, who'd drawn a hobnailed leather chair close to the fire, held open a dark green book with a bold gold title. The story that she read aloud teemed with heroic gods, beautiful goddesses, and mythical babies with wings.

Much to his dismay, Throckmorton's body was propped on the rug against the back of the dead bear's head, a truly grisly state of affairs. Making matters worse, Throckmorton's long skinny tail was trapped beneath a bloodhound's muzzle.

He certainly hoped that the dog, whose name

was Bailey, wouldn't slobber. (Sock monkeys simply despise dog slobber.)

Miss Pine unexpectedly closed the book. "Annaliese, would you like me to tell you a story?"

"What kind of story?"

"A pirate story."

"Sure," Annaliese replied.

Yay hooray!

Throckmorton loved pirate stories . . . especially if they were true.

Once, he'd heard the maid, Madge, tell Annaliese that a hundred something years ago, Henry Easterling had had unscrupulous dealings with pirates. And that gold doubloons and crown jewels were stashed to this day somewhere inside Eastcliff's walls.

Miss Pine's clear voice interrupted Throckmorton's wandering thoughts. "Among the swashbuckling pirates who swarmed the dangerous seas of the North Atlantic," she began, "none was more vicious than Mallory Smyth."

With a wicked gleam in her eye, she curled the ends of an imaginary mustache. "Mallory Smyth left no survivors . . . 'Dead cats,' he boasted, 'don't meow.'"

Miss Pine was just getting to the good part when Teddy strutted in, holding a sock monkey—Captain

Eugene!—above his head like a trophy.

Throckmorton wanted to shout, "Ahoy there, mate!" to his nautically dressed cousin, but he didn't dare, not when persons of the human persuasion were within earshot.

(Like all sock monkeys, Throckmorton believed that disaster would strike if a keeper ever heard his or her sock monkey speak.)

"Where'd you find him?" asked Annaliese.

"None of your business," her brother answered. Grinning, he placed Captain Eugene, who was much smaller than Throckmorton, on Bailey's liver-colored back.

Unlike Throckmorton, Captain Eugene looked ever-so-dapper in a gold-braided navy captain's hat and a peacoat with tiny brass buttons.

Upon closer inspection, Throckmorton noticed that his cousin's limbs were badly stained in some places and completely worn thin in others. Clearly, Teddy's sock monkey had been well-loved for a long, long time—not trapped in a foul-smelling net!

Throckmorton could almost feel his stuffing turn green.

A deep, dark shade of jealous green.

"I wonder why Great-Grandmama gave us sock monkeys," said Annaliese. "Why not teddy bears? Or puppets?"

"What I want to know is why Great-Grandmama made Father a girl monkey," said Evan, who'd slunk into the library empty-handed. "Boys should get boy monkeys and girls should get girl monkeys."

Annaliese drew Throckmorton into her arms, rescuing him from beasts both dead and alive. "My sock monkey's a boy," she said proudly. "And I'd never, ever trade him for a girl."

Alleluia! Throckmorton rejoiced, relaxing into her embrace.

Evan slumped into the armchair closest to the snapping, crackling fire. "I've searched the main rooms on the first floor, the cellar, and some of the bedrooms on the second floor too. We should also search the east and west wings, but Father has the keys."

"You'd better not disturb him," Teddy warned. "You know how he gets . . ."

"Father gets horrible headaches at night," Annaliese explained to Miss Pine.

"Like lightning striking between his ears," said Teddy.

Miss Pine, who suddenly appeared weary, eased herself out of the leather chair. "Well, don't forget the attic—that's where most unwanted toys end up."

"We're not allowed to go in the attic," Teddy explained. "It's one of Father's rules."

Annaliese tossed her head and then flipped the ends of her plaits. "Like wearing braids."

The gilded bronze mantel clock chimed nine times. "Well, mates, let's call off the search party, shall we?" suggested Miss Pine. "It's bedtime."

"Another one of Father's stupid rules," Evan moaned. "Bedtime's for babies."

Throckmorton, however, sighed with relief.

Bedtime, at last . . . the end of a tumultuous day . . . a mighty turn of events that required serious mulling over.

But tonight?

Tonight, all Throckmorton wanted was to lie in Annaliese's arms and dream about the great party to come.

And he did.

Rumors and Relatives

Huddled under Annaliese's bedcovers, Throckmorton traveled in his mind back to those long-ago and faraway nights when Olivia made up silly little rhymes that she sang until he and Baby Annaliese fell to sleep:

Sock monkey, Throck-monkey, rock-around-the-clock monkey . . .

And he dreamed he was dancing beneath a crystal chandelier brimming with light.

Throck-monkey, sock monkey, hockey-stick-and-puck-monkey . . .

And he saw himself skating down a silver river of sparkling ice.

Sock monkey, Throck-monkey, lobster-in-the-pot-monkey . . .

And he became as strong as fishermen who draw crusty-shelled creatures out of the sea.

Olivia's make-believe music had always given Throckmorton hope.

Hope that someday, he'd dance and do cartwheels.

Hope that some way, he'd skip and turn somersaults.

Hope that one day, he'd stand on his own two feet.

When he woke up the next morning, Annaliese carried him down to breakfast by his tail. Throckmorton was ever-so-grateful. Hanging upside down scrambled his brains just the way he liked them.

She wedged his body between a toaster and a cookie jar. The kitchen counter provided a perfect spot for eavesdropping and spying—skills at which he excelled.

In the alcove breakfast nook, Annaliese, Evan, and Teddy sat on wooden benches staring at empty bowls.

Mrs. Wiggins, the family's kind but cantankerous cook, stood at the stove stirring hot cereal in a copper pot. Mrs. Wiggins and her husband, Max, the stable keeper, had faithfully served four generations of Easterlings.

Annaliese's brothers were twins, but they didn't look alike. Teddy's dark curly hair resembled a choppy sea. Evan's hair looked like a bristle—reddish-brown with a stubborn cowlick near the center of his hairline.

Annaliese's always-braided hair was thick and crinkly, a mixture of quiet brown and creamy blond strands, not unlike the color of Throckmorton's wooly skin. Her aunties called the color "odd."

Annaliese had her mother's eyes: sometimes blue,

sometimes green, sometimes gray—a moody color, like the sea, ever changing depending on the light.

When the telephone rang, the judge, with newspaper in hand, hurried into the kitchen past Mrs. Wiggins to answer it.

"Good morning, Ray." He drew back a checkered window curtain. "You could be right—it does look like a snowstorm's heading this way."

Quickly, the topic turned from Maine's wintry weather to Great-Grandmama Easterling's surprising invitation.

"What's she up to? I have no idea. . . . ," said the judge. "It's her birthday. When you're as old and rich and quirky as she is, well, I guess you can throw yourself any kind of party you like . . . No, I don't know why she invited the sock monkeys. . . . Why Ray, that's crazy! I'm sure it has nothing to do with what's in Great-Grandmama's will. . . . Yes, I'll call you back."

The judge set the receiver back in its cradle.

"Sounds like your brother-in-law is stirring up trouble again," clucked Mrs. Wiggins.

The judge kneaded the deep crease in his forehead. "Ray said that my sister Pansy said that Cousin Willie said that this whole sock monkey business has something to do with Great-Grandmama's will: 'No monkey, no money.'"

"No monkey, no money . . . what's that supposed to mean?" asked Evan.

"If you don't bring your sock monkey to the party, she'll cut you out of her will?" Mrs. Wiggins guessed.

"Did you find Sir Rudyard yet?" Teddy asked Evan.

Evan shook his head.

"Don't ask me where Sir Rudyard might be," said Mrs. Wiggins. "For all I know, he's been cut into rags."

Cut into rags?

Throckmorton shuddered. In his mind he pictured that lazy maid Madge polishing the banister with his cousin's body parts, whistling while she worked.

"I can't believe that my own grandmother would cut me out of her will," the judge griped, "if I don't bring an old sock monkey to her birthday party."

"If you don't bring Miss Beatrice," Annaliese clarified.

Evan's eyes widened. "You mean that I'm not going to get any of Great-Grandmama's swell stuff because I can't find a stupid sock monkey named Sir Rudyard?"

Old sock monkey?

Stupid sock monkey?

If Throckmorton could've, he would've thrown father and son into that hot copper pot and turned up the heat.

"It's not fair!" Evan ranted. "Great-Grandmama promised that I could have the sword in the scabbard above the fireplace. And the bearskin rug and the . . ."

"Son, we're not just talking about swords and skins here, we're talking about the Easterling family fortune."

With a resounding *bra-aanngg!* Mrs. Wiggins clanged a steel lid down on her pot. "Ingrates," she said under her breath. "The whole lot of you."

The cook's eyes glazed with angry tears.

"All . . . all . . . Ethel wants . . . ," she stammered, "is, um, to see all of you . . . one more time before . . . well, you know."

A moment of stunned silence followed. Mrs. Wiggins lifted her eyes heavenward. She fingered the bead rosary that she typically kept in her apron pocket.

"Is Great-Grandmama dying?" Teddy asked.

Annaliese looked stricken. "She is?"

"Not that I know of," the judge replied. "What Mrs. Wiggins was trying to say is that Great-Grandmama is getting on in years. She wants to see us all together again."

"Oh, like a family reunion," said Annaliese.

"Sounds like she wants to see her sock monkeys a whole lot more than she does any of us," Teddy observed.

Truer words might never have been spoken, thought Throckmorton. The Easterlings were a contentious bunch, petty and always fighting about something—possessions sometimes, but usually money.

"I'm not taking any chances," Evan decided, sliding off the bench. "Come on! We've got to find Sir Rudyard NOW."

"And Miss Beatrice," added the judge, who'd taken a chair at the outer edge of the table.

Annaliese and Teddy scrambled to their feet.

"Let's go!" Teddy cried.

Mrs. Wiggins brandished her wooden spoon. "Wait! Your breakfast is ready."

"We're not hungry!" Evan, Teddy, and Annaliese responded in unison.

From behind the pages of the *Rock County Courier*, the judge ordered, "Eat your porridge."

The children stopped cold, slid back onto the benches, and ate.

Soon a second phone call distracted the judge.

The cook motioned for the children to look her way, nodding and winking as though to convey something very secret.

Mrs. Wiggins opened the cupboard door right above Throckmorton's head. She pried off the lid of a tin coffee can, painted red with a ship sailing at sunset, and pulled out a ring of keys of various shapes and sizes.

"You'll need a key," she whispered to Evan, holding the largest key between her pinched fingers. "To the attic." She pointed toward the pantry. "And flashlights."

Evan swiped the ring of keys out of the cook's hand. Teddy dashed into the pantry.

Evan raised his arm until it was as straight as a sword.

"To the attic," he commanded, mouthing the words. *"Tout de suite!"*

Good Riddance!

Oh, how Throckmorton hated being left behind between the toaster and the cookie jar, legs splayed, limp and helpless. Adding insult to injury, a bit of porridge flew from the cook's wooden spoon and landed—*splat!*—on his button eye.

Phooey, phooey, fiddlesticks!

Throckmorton's day was not getting off to a good start.

Nor was the judge's.

Eastcliff's telephone simply wouldn't stop ringing.

Apparently the "no monkey, no money" rumor had skipped across phone lines like squirrels in a hurry. Relatives to whom Judge Easterling hadn't spoken in years called to ask: "Is it true?"

Brriinngg . . . Brriinngg . . .

Mrs. Wiggins picked up the phone, but the judge grabbed the receiver out of her hand.

"Hello?"

Above the bridge of his nose, the judge's eyebrows grew together. "I'm sorry to hear that," he said.

"Yes, I had planned to use up some of my vacation time." His face was tense. "But I had no intention of going anywhere—and certainly not abroad."

The judge rocked on his heels, frowning.

Meanwhile, Mrs. Wiggins was all ears.

"Tonight?" he exclaimed. "But you know that Mother and I don't get along. I can't possibly . . ."

Uh-oh . . . Throckmorton didn't like the sound of this.

"All right, I will," the judge answered brusquely.

Now his mustache was really twitching. "Yes, I promise."

"Well?" Mrs. Wiggins probed after he hung up.

"That was the birthday girl," he responded sarcastically. "I'm to go to London at once. Mother's health has taken a turn for the worse."

The judge's mother, a widow named Margaret, was Great-Grandmama's daughter-in-law, a semi-invalid whom Throckmorton had never seen before.

"I'm sorry to hear that," Mrs. Wiggins replied.

"It's Mother's arthritis," he explained, pacing back and forth. "She can't travel alone. I'm to accompany her and Madame Something S. Monkey back to East-cliff in time for Great-Grandmama's birthday party."

"Oh, sure, now I remember," the cook said. "Dame Lorraine S. Monkey was your father's sock monkey. In John's will, he left Dame Lorraine to your mother." Mrs. Wiggins smiled. "Dame Lorraine was quite the beauty in her day: diamond earrings, a triple strand of pearls, and a real mink stole."

Throckmorton perked his ears.

A jeweled sock monkey with a real mink stole?

Adorned with nothing but a diaper pin, Throckmorton felt belittled in the face of such extravagance.

Perhaps he shouldn't have been surprised. Annaliese's absent grandmother Margaret was one of the reasons that Annaliese's bedroom was festooned with toys she didn't play with and clothes she rarely wore. Margaret was always sending new gifts from London's finest stores.

The judge's shoulders sagged. "The arrangements have all been made. I'll be leaving late this afternoon."

"Terrible time to be traveling," Mrs. Wiggins said with scant sincerity. "And, such a strange coincidence . . . what with the P sisters showing up any day now to help plan the party."

The judge had seven older sisters. All their names began with the letter *P*.

The judge drew his head back swiftly. "Who told you that?"

Mrs. Wiggins stuck a loose hairpin back into the silver bun that she wore coiled above the nape of her neck. "News travels fast."

The judge scrubbed his face with his hands and mumbled something about Great-Grandmama playing him like a fiddle. Then he spied the enormous dog named Donald lying on a braided rug just inside the pantry.

He took a deep breath and let it out slowly. "If I've told you once, Mrs. Wiggins," he roared, "I've told you a thousand times. *That* dog stays outside where he belongs."

Donald had been Olivia's dog, a huge harlequin-patterned Great Dane that she'd left behind when he was just a puppy.

Throckmorton considered Donald to be living proof that Annaliese's mother had always meant to return. He didn't care what anyone said: Olivia had loved her children and her dog.

Someone or something awful had prevented her return.

When it came to the Great Dane, Mrs. Wiggins knew better than to argue. "Out you go, Donald."

Throckmorton heard the *click-click-click* of the Great Dane's toenails as the gentle, ungainly beast crossed the kitchen's well-scrubbed floor. Waiting at the back door, the poor dog appeared to have resigned himself to his fate: a choke collar and long chain, anchored to a tall tree.

"So I suppose I'd better start packing," said the judge.

Mrs. Wiggins turned her back on her employer.

"The sooner the better, I always say."

As the judge's footsteps trailed away, Mrs. Wiggins scraped the sticky morsel out of Throckmorton's eye.

"Good riddance," she muttered under her breath.

Did Mrs. Wiggins mean the porridge or the judge? Throckmorton wondered.

The cook put her arm into the sleeve of her winter coat. She heaved an exasperated sigh. "Don't worry, dear," she told the dog. "I'll bring you back inside as soon as he's gone."

Good riddance, indeed!

In all honesty, Throckmorton didn't like Judge Easterling.

He never had.

And he was pretty sure he never would.

No, not after what happened one summer when Annaliese was about four years old . . .

In those days, Throckmorton fondly recalled, he and Annaliese were inseparable. His little keeper dragged him wherever she went until his tail frayed and the threads on the bottoms of his feet shredded.

One blistering hot and humid afternoon, Evan, Teddy, and Annaliese were scouring the attic in search of costumes for a re-creation of *The Three Billy Goats Gruff.*

Throckmorton was out of sorts at the time. Annaliese had suggested that her brothers look for tiny sets of horns so that their sock monkeys might play the parts of grumpy goats . . . a humiliating way to spend a day if there ever was one.

"Where's *your* sock monkey?" she asked Evan. "We need three goats."

Throckmorton wondered the same thing. He hadn't seen Evan play with Sir Rudyard for a long, long time.

"I don't know where he is." Evan shrugged. "Lost, I guess."

After looking around for a few minutes, he dragged a big box, filled with old toys, out of the corner. He pulled out a badly beat-up bear and tossed it to his sister. "Here, this guy will work."

Shortly before they left the attic, Teddy discovered a golden crocodile-leather suitcase filled with women's clothing. After pillaging its contents, he held a silky fringed shawl, shimmering with color, up to the light.

"Do you think that any of this stuff belongs to our mother?" he asked loudly.

Evan glared at his twin. He pointed at Annaliese and then drew a line across his lips.

Too late.

"We don't have a mother," Annaliese retorted.

"We do too, silly," Teddy told her. "Everyone has a mother. Even us."

Annaliese stomped her foot. "Do not!"

"Do so," Teddy repeated. "You just don't remember her."

With her eyes, Annaliese begged for Evan to disagree.

He didn't.

Annaliese gathered Throckmorton into her arms and bolted down the attic stairs. Back in her bedroom, she soaked his body with her tears, precious medals of high honor that he wore proudly to this day.

A few hours later, when Judge Easterling came home from work, Annaliese ambushed him at the front door. Her cheeks were burning and her chin trembled.

"What happened to my mother?" Annaliese demanded. "Where is she? What was her name?"

"I don't know." The judge set his jaw. "Where she is, I mean."

"I don't believe you!" Annaliese wailed.

Anger seethed beneath his next words. "What I do know is that your mother had a gypsy's spirit and she ran away with a man with a pirate's heart."

How wild and scary and romantic, Throckmorton had thought at the time . . . and oh, what a terrible,

terrible truth for a four-year-old child to be told.

"And that's all I intend to say about her—now, or ever."

Annaliese tried to ask another question, but the judge crossed his arms in front of his chest. He glared at her with fiery eyes. "See that you do the same."

Throckmorton never heard Annaliese or her brothers speak about their mother again. The judge locked the attic, and although the children often looked, they never found the key.

Silence and secrets . . .

Secrets and silence . . .

Throckmorton had never forgiven the heartless man.

Didn't Judge Easterling realize that sweet Annaliese knew nothing about the dangers and dark sides of love?

No, Throckmorton didn't like the judge.

Not now.

Not ever.

A Map of the Past

Before Throckmorton had any more time to ponder the sad past, Annaliese and Teddy returned to the kitchen. Annaliese was bundled in a wool coat with a fur collar, fur muff, and matching fur hat. A cobweb hung from the hat's brim like a torn veil. Captain Eugene was perched on Teddy's shoulder.

"It's freezing up there," Annaliese told Mrs. Wiggins. "We came downstairs to get our sock monkeys. We're hoping they'll bring us good luck."

"We passed Father on the staircase," Teddy said. "He didn't look too happy."

The cook shrugged.

"Thanks for giving us the keys, Mrs. Wiggins." Annaliese's face brightened. "Our attic is like a giant treasure chest."

Mrs. Wiggins picked up a dish towel and shooed them off.

Annaliese and Throckmorton trailed Teddy and Captain Eugene past Eastcliff's ballroom on the third floor and then up the narrow stairs to the attic on the fourth floor. Bailey—a trained scent hound with weak eyes and a bad hip—soldiered loyally behind.

Anxiety about the fate of his missing cousins caused Throckmorton's stuffing to clump.

What if moths had munched hundreds of holes in Sir Rudyard's woolly skin?

What if a mouse had burrowed into Miss Beatrice's body, set up housekeeping, and given birth to nine babies?

Or what if his cousins—deprived of human touch for such a long, long time—had completely lost their senses?

Throckmorton cringed, recalling Annaliese's store-bought stuffed animals that couldn't see, couldn't hear, couldn't think, and couldn't feel.

Inside the attic's main room, the air was dry and musty. Morning light shone dull and gray through grimy windowpanes. Shadows lurked in cluttered corners and ghostly white bed sheets covered hulking pieces of furniture.

Everything smelled lonely.

Annaliese and Teddy tucked their sock monkeys into a wicker baby buggy with rusty wheels and then plunged into the attic's dimly lit interior. Bailey tagged along.

"Evan! We're back!" Teddy called. "Did you find anything?"

"Nope!"

Throckmorton scanned the array of castoffs

deadened by dust: antlers, arrows, and alligator purses; bowlers and beaver hats; fans, furs, and stuffed seagulls; jump ropes, jacks, and jigsaw puzzles; mustard jars and Merry Christmas mugs; a weather vane, wind chimes, and an old Victrola.

How would the children ever find the missing sock monkeys in such a muddled mess?

"I fear the worst," Throckmorton told Captain Eugene, once Teddy and Annaliese were out of earshot.

"Aye, I do as well," said the captain. "I haven't seen Sir Rudyard in years—not since Evan was a tyke."

"By the way, where were you?" Throckmorton asked. "It didn't take Teddy very long to find you."

"That's because," his cousin explained, "I was never lost."

"You weren't?"

"Oh, my heavens, no," said Captain Eugene. "It's just that, well . . . Master Teddy keeps me well hidden." He lowered his voice. "I think he's afraid that Evan or Judge Easterling will tease him if they discover that he's still so fond of me."

"They surely would," Throckmorton agreed.

"Teddy hides me inside his marble pouch. Or I hang upside down, bat-style, in the corner behind a globe. Sometimes I nap underneath the skivvies in his dresser drawer."

"That's terrible," Throckmorton commiserated.

"There are worse fates," Captain Eugene responded matter-of-factly. "Besides, every night without fail Teddy takes off my hat, unbuttons my jacket, folds it up neatly, and tucks me inside his pillowcase. The lad's never slept without me. I don't know what he'll do when . . ."

Captain Eugene's voice cracked.

"When what?" asked Throckmorton.

"Haven't you heard? The judge is sending Evan and Teddy to boarding school."

A queasy, uneasy feeling spread across Throckmorton's body. "Annaliese too?"

"Oh no," Captain Eugene answered. "I overheard Annaliese ask Judge Easterling if she could attend as well. He told her that St. John's Military Academy is for boys only. Miss Pine will be Annaliese's tutor as well as her nanny."

Throckmorton was relieved that Annaliese would remain at Eastcliff. Still, she must have found the news terribly upsetting.

Not that Evan and Teddy played with their little sister that often anymore . . . but she didn't have any friends. And, no matter how many times she'd asked him, Judge Easterling wouldn't let her attend the local school. It was an awfully lonely existence for a nine-year-old girl.

"What about Teddy?" Throckmorton asked. "Does he want to go?"

"Absolutely not!" Captain Eugene declared.

After a moment Throckmorton said softly, "When are they leaving?"

Captain Eugene hesitated, as if reluctant to seal the truth with his answer. "The day after Great-Grandmama's birthday party."

A mournful silence followed.

Throckmorton didn't know what to say or do to comfort his grief-stricken cousin. Every sock monkey fears the day when his or her keeper heads off into a wide, wide world far beyond a sock monkey's imagination.

Now, as Evan, Teddy, and Annaliese searched the terrain of their family's past, their pillaging and plundering became more frantic.

Wooden crates scraped over plank flooring. Bird cages rattled. Bells rang. Hinges squeaked as the children pried open lids of steamer trunks. Pencil cases spilled. Baskets tipped. Arrowheads, seashells, pins, buttons, and lots of itty-bitty things scattered.

When a stack of shoe boxes toppled over, Evan yelled, "Timmmm-berrrr!" as if he'd sawed down a tall tree.

Moments later, Teddy burst through a clothes rack laden with garment bags. Cheeks red and teeth chattering, he declared, "I—I—I give up!"

"No, wait! I've got an idea," said Annaliese, who'd been busily pairing shoes to put back into the right boxes.

"I've got a better one," Teddy responded. "Let's go downstairs."

Annaliese stood up and slapped her thigh. "Here, Bailey!" she called.

Skeptical looks crossed her brothers' faces.

Bailey's eyes lit up. The gloomy dog with droopy ears waddled toward her, ready and eager to report for duty.

Swoosh!

Before Throckmorton knew what hit him, he was dangling upside down in front of the dog's wrinkled, whiskered face.

"Look, Bailey."

Annaliese wiggled and juggled Throckmorton's body like some pathetic puppet. "See? Sock monkey."

What his keeper did next was unthinkable, almost unforgivable: She rubbed Throckmorton's bare red bottom back and forth across the dog's cold wet nose.

The beast sniffed.

He snuffled.

He slobbered.

"Oooh, wet . . ." Throckmorton recoiled at the sheer indignity of it all.

"Go. Find. Sock. Monkey," Annaliese ordered.

Evan scoffed. "As if that worthless bloodhound could sniff out a couple of sock monkeys . . ."

"Sherlock Holmes might disagree," Teddy observed wryly.

Scenting an invisible trail, Bailey zigzagged away. Soon a resounding bay rang through the rafters. "Ah-rooooooo!"

Evan and Teddy exchanged looks of disbelief.

"He's on to something!" Annaliese cried, turning Throckmorton right side up. "Let's go!"

The hound's bellowing came from behind a tall golden harp, partly covered with a black drape secured by a length of gold tasseled cord.

"Give me a hand," Annaliese yelled.

Evan and Teddy inched the harp away from the wall. Punctuating the air with their grunts, they shoved Olivia's once-beloved instrument aside.

Bailey feverishly scored the wall boards with his long, strong toenails. Evan beamed his flashlight up, down, and around the wall. Then he ran his hands over a panel of wood wider and newer looking than the others.

"It's some kind of makeshift door," he said.

Annaliese bounced from foot to foot. "Open it! Open it!"

Teddy crossed his fingers. "Maybe this is where the gold doubloons and crown jewels are stashed."

The panel bore simple hinges but no handle. In the darkish light, its small keyhole—almost invisible unless you knew where to look—might have been mistaken for a knothole.

Evan pulled the cook's ring of keys out of his coat pocket. He shifted his eyes from keyhole to keys, sizing them up.

After a few wrong guesses, *voila!*

A key turned, the lock clicked.

Evan poked the panel with two fingers. Creaking eerily, the door opened into a pitch-black space— the kind of space, Throckmorton feared, that was best left undisturbed.

Buried Alive

The hidden room had no windows. Inside, the blackness was so foreboding that Bailey stopped dead in his tracks, his tail taut and curved like a sickle. A low growl gurgled in his throat, as if spirits whispered warnings that only dogs could hear.

The three children bunched together in front of the open door.

Beams from Evan's flashlight illuminated the room's angled ceiling and narrow rectangular shape. Cobwebs formed a flimsy canopy above an assortment of black instrument cases, music stands, an upright piano, and a couple of chairs.

"It feels like a graveyard," Annaliese whispered.

"The sock monkeys won't be in there," said Teddy. "Plus you're right, Annaliese, the room is creepy."

"Sissy," Evan taunted, yet didn't step forward himself.

"Come on," Annaliese urged. She gripped Throckmorton's neck with a firm hand and boldly crossed the threshold.

"I've got this feeling . . ."

She probed the sinister darkness, sweeping away the cobwebs with an outstretched hand. Throckmorton cringed, anticipating a shower of spiders, or an explosion of angry bats whose roost they'd so rudely invaded.

Annaliese patted the tallest and widest instrument case. "Evan, shine the light this way," she called.

Never one to be outdone by his little sister, Evan bolted into the room. "Here, let me," he said, nudging her aside.

Evan grabbed the handle, unsnapped three brass latches, and opened the broad lid. He steadied the cumbersome case to show her what lay inside: a double bass fiddle.

He plucked a few strings and closed the lid.

Teddy, who'd followed Evan into the spooky room, opened the second largest case: a cello.

Then the eye of Evan's flashlight revealed a drum set as well as a stout square case lying in the corner. "An accordion, maybe?"

"It's like a band left behind all of its instruments," said Annaliese.

"See, I told you," Teddy said. "No sock monkeys."

Annaliese scratched her temple. "What kind of a band would hide their instruments here?"

"And why?" questioned Evan.

Throckmorton was pretty sure he knew who had left the instruments behind. But he had no idea why.

Suddenly, Bailey let out an agitated yelp and started to frantically paw at the handle of a violin case.

Annaliese tucked Throckmorton tightly under her left arm. She drew the small case out of the dog's reach. "This one's not very heavy."

She gave the case a shake. No sound. No rattle.

She shifted it from side to side, set it on top of the accordion case, and then lifted the lid.

Annaliese's mouth fell open. "Bailey was right!"

Evan shined the light on the contents of the violin case. His brow furrowed.

"It's Sir Rudyard, that's for sure," Teddy said. "Don't tell me, Evan, that you don't remember him."

Annaliese adjusted Throckmorton's body so that he could see inside.

Immediately he wished that she hadn't.

Mercy, mercy, mercy . . .

Wedged into the irregularly shaped space, Sir Rudyard's body contorted, flattening his face. In the neck of the case, his fingerless hands pressed together as if in prayer, his once-smiling red mouth shaped like a scream.

"What's my sock monkey doing inside a violin case?" Evan shook his head, glancing around as if

looking for answers. "It makes no sense."

"Probably one of Madge's stupid tricks," Teddy suggested.

Evan cupped his hand around the back of Sir Rudyard's head. He started to ease his sock monkey out of the case, but Teddy stopped him.

"Take the case, too," he told his brother. "Maybe there's a clue inside."

"Good thinking." Evan slammed the lid. "That's three down, one to go."

"Let's come back later." Teddy rubbed the palms of his gloves together. "I'm freezing."

"Hold on . . ." Annaliese sneezed. "Look, there's one more." She waved her hanky at a small case leaning against the back wall.

Throckmorton hoped that they'd find the pear-shaped case empty. He couldn't bear to see another sock monkey in such a deplorable state.

Evan peeked under the arched lid. He grinned.

"Is it Miss Beatrice?" Annaliese asked.

Evan gave Teddy and Annaliese a thumbs-up. "Four for four! We're in the money," he declared. "Let's go!"

"I can't wait to tell Father," Annaliese said.

"No," Evan said angrily. "Not until I say it's okay."

"Why?" she asked.

"There's something fishy going on." He swept

his arm over the musical graveyard. "None of this makes any sense."

"That's for sure." Teddy nodded.

Evan backed out of the hidden room with the two instrument cases in hand. Teddy and Annaliese followed.

"Listen, we need to get our stories straight," said Evan darkly, "until our investigation is complete."

He raised his index finger. "One, we found the sock monkeys in a closet." He lifted his middle finger. "Two, there's no hidden room."

"And, three . . ." He flashed three fingers. "No abandoned instrument cases."

Annaliese slowly shook her head. "I don't want to get in any trouble . . ."

"You won't," Evan told her. "Trust me."

While Evan and Teddy pressed the panel door back into place, Annaliese poked her head into a dark recess behind the harp.

Something caught her attention, but Throckmorton couldn't see what.

"Come on, Annaliese," Teddy called out. "We're ready to lock up."

Teddy retrieved Captain Eugene on their way out of the attic. "We found your cousins!" he told his sock monkey.

Sadly, Throckmorton imagined how Captain

Eugene's heart would break when he laid his eyes on Sir Rudyard.

Evan locked the attic door at the bottom of the narrow staircase.

"I'll go down the back way," Evan said. "Let's meet in my room in ten minutes."

Annaliese opened her hand. "Mrs. Wiggins will want her keys back."

Evan tossed her the ring. "If she asks, tell her that we're still looking. Remember, mum's the word."

Evan and Teddy walked off in different directions, but Annaliese lingered. She set Throckmorton in a side chair and then bent over, unbuckling and buckling her Mary Jane shoes.

From where he sat, Throckmorton spied Madge down the hall, near the ballroom's double doors. Her back was to them.

Madge, who was pushing a carpet sweeper, stopped to open the door of a massive curio cabinet filled with a rare collection of tiny, intricately carved ivory animals. She stuck her hand in, grabbed one of the priceless miniatures, and dropped it into her apron pocket.

Annaliese looked up, but too late to see the maid's petty theft.

"That Madge," she said, wrinkling her nose.

"She's always lurking somewhere."

To this day, Throckmorton could still smell Madge's foul breath and fishy-smelling hands at the moment she'd tossed him into the net.

He'd always despised the lazy maid, but he'd never dreamed that she was a thief to boot.

Once Madge disappeared, Annaliese unlocked the attic door and dashed back up to the fourth floor. She sprinted toward the door to the hidden room, squeezed past the harp, and scrambled into the alcove.

Now Throckmorton could see what had earlier captured Annaliese's attention: a steamer trunk, a row of suitcases, and a stack of hat and dress boxes.

Without hesitation, she grabbed a medium-sized piece of luggage. Throckmorton recognized the suitcase right away: It was golden and made of crocodile leather.

He thought back to that sorrowful afternoon five years earlier, when Teddy had opened the very same suitcase. Teddy's innocent question replayed in Throckmorton's mind: *Do you think that any of this stuff belongs to our mother?*

Throckmorton had never forgotten the answer.

And now he knew that Annaliese hadn't either.

Annaliese stashed the golden crocodile suitcase under her bed. Then she left her bedroom briefly, returning with a large flat box. She slid the box, with curved silver letters drawn on its cover, next to the suitcase.

She gripped Throckmorton in one hand and the ring of keys in the other and rushed down to the kitchen. When Mrs. Wiggins asked if they'd found the missing sock monkeys, Annaliese answered, "We're still looking," like a loyal soldier.

She reported to Evan's bedroom, armed with a secret of her own. She placed Throckmorton next to Captain Eugene on the leather seat of a rolling desk chair.

Dismal, water-stained wallpaper—a pattern of ferns, dark green and drooping—covered Evan's bedroom walls. Heavy drapes blocked the rare rays of winter sun. His collection of miniature lead soldiers covered the shelves and surfaces of every piece of furniture.

Throckmorton sighed. How unhappy the tiny warriors' painted faces appeared . . . how hard their minuscule hearts must be . . .

Evan and Teddy lay on the floor with their arms beneath their heads, waiting to open the violin and mandolin cases. Bailey was stretched out next to Teddy, straining to keep one eye open. Annaliese dropped to her knees and joined the circle.

Her brothers sat up at the same time. Evan claimed the violin case, which had three latches. Teddy's fingers hovered above the two latches on the mandolin case.

"Ready . . . Set . . . Go!" said Evan, followed by a series of rapid snaps.

Despair tore at Throckmorton's heart as he viewed the bodies of his cousins lying lifeless before him. He'd heard the horror stories before, of course. But never had he witnessed firsthand what happens to sock monkeys who've been unloved for a long, long time.

The symptoms of long-term abandonment were unmistakable.

Sir Rudyard's glass eyes didn't focus. His ears sagged. The woven threads of his sock face had lost their elasticity.

Miss Beatrice was balled up inside the mandolin case's oval, velvet-lined interior. She wore an ivory satin dress. A tulle veil, attached to a broken crown of dried flowers, covered her squashed, lumpy face. Her eyelashes were like Throckmorton's: slashes of black embroidery thread. Her jingle-bell eyes registered not even a sliver of sight.

Throckmorton and Captain Eugene exchanged worried glances, flicks of movement imperceptible to the human eye.

Why had their cousins been sentenced to such a loveless existence? Would they ever—*could* they ever—recover?

Evan sat up, eased Sir Rudyard into a standing position, and met his sock monkey eye to eye. Evan's face, usually stony and pale, softened. "Why don't I remember you?" he asked.

Throckmorton crossed his imaginary fingers, hoping that by the magic of his keeper's touch, Sir Rudyard would emit even a tiny spark of sock monkey soul.

"I think that you owe Sir Rudyard an apology," Annaliese told Evan. "Tell him that you're sorry you forgot about him. That's what I did, and Throckmorton's completely forgiven me."

And indeed, Throckmorton had. (Red-heeled sock monkeys, sewn by hand and stitched with love, find it almost impossible to carry a grudge.)

"Wait a minute . . . ," said Teddy, who'd lifted homely Miss Beatrice out of the mandolin case. "What's that?"

"What's what?" asked Annaliese.

Teddy reached into the bottom of the case. He fished out a thin gold-link chain and dangled it from his fingers. "A necklace, I guess, with a pendant."

Holy moley!

It wasn't just any old necklace—it was Olivia's locket!

Teddy handed the locket to Evan, who let Sir Rudyard collapse.

From a desk drawer Evan removed a magnifying glass worthy of Sherlock Holmes. He positioned it above the jeweled face of a small gold sphere.

"Diamonds, I think, and a ruby." He pinched open the halves of the ornamental case and squinted. "With two tiny portraits inside."

After several seconds of silence, Evan passed the magnifying glass and locket back to Teddy. "Here, take a look."

Teddy peered at the miniature portraits. His face whitened.

"You remember her, don't you?" Evan asked him.

Teddy nodded solemnly.

"Her?" asked Annaliese.

"Our mother," Evan answered.

"Our *mother*?" she shrieked. "Our mother?"

"For gosh sakes, Annaliese," said Teddy, "lower your voice."

Teddy pressed the locket and magnifying glass into her outstretched hands. "See for yourself."

"Who else would it be?" Evan said. "That's Father without his mustache; there, on the left."

"She looks so young," said Annaliese.

"Eighteen when Father married her," Evan replied.

"I didn't know that," said Annaliese.

Teddy dropped his chin. He bit on his lower lip and ran his hand up and down Bailey's back.

Tension rippled across Throckmorton's chest. If he'd had breath to hold, he would've held it.

Annaliese's lips quivered. "She's—she's—she's just like I imagined her to be . . . like I know her," she said. "Like I've always known her."

"Know her, schmow her," Evan snarled, snatching the locket out of her hand. "She may as well be dead for all she cares about us."

"She *must* care about us!" Annaliese insisted.

"No. She doesn't." Evan snapped the locket shut. "Never has. Never will."

Throckmorton now watched with horror as Teddy's hands formed into fists. His lips moved back and forth, contorting his cheeks.

Ptew! A mouthful of Teddy's spit grazed Evan's face.

Stunned and caught off guard, Evan's head

sprung back. The locket skidded out of his hand. An instant later, he lunged forward and dug his fingers deep into Teddy's neck.

"Stop it! Stop it!" Annaliese screamed.

Teddy elbowed Evan's chest and twisted out of his clutches.

The bedroom door flung open and the judge thundered into Evan's room. "What the devil's going on in here?"

With a sleight of hand, Evan whisked the locket under his leg.

The judge's stormy gray eyes shifted back and forth between the open instrument cases and the sock monkeys lying on the rug. "The three of you have some explaining to do."

Annaliese offered Miss Beatrice up to the judge. "Look, Father, we found your sock monkey."

The judge grabbed Miss Beatrice by the head, crushing the veil's flowered crown in his grip.

At that very moment, Miss Pine dashed into the room.

The judge wheeled round upon her. "Miss Pine," he growled, "I told you once and I'm not telling you again." His voice rose to a roar. "Take care of this monkey business!"

"Meaning, sir?"

"Meaning, remove Miss Beatrice's ridiculous

dress, it's not hers. And, keep her under wraps until I return."

"Yes, sir."

"Our future depends on it!"

The judge stomped out of the room. Miss Pine stood as if frozen for a few seconds. Then she darted after him, plaintively calling, "Judge Easterling! Please, may I have a word?"

Evan, Teddy, and Annaliese re-formed their circle. Teddy and Annaliese's faces were crestfallen; Evan looked close to tears.

Although their mother's portrait was no bigger than a thumbprint, the locket was a vivid, bitter reminder that Olivia was a living, breathing human being—real enough to have once lived in this unhappy house—real enough to have packed up and left.

Throckmorton felt all spongy and unsettled inside. He realized anew how difficult the children's lives had been.

Waiting and wondering, wondering and waiting . . . all traces of their mother's existence swept out of sight.

Evan moved his leg, revealing the locket.

"May I have it?" Annaliese asked with a tremor in her voice. "Please?"

Evan wiped his nose with the back of his hand. "No."

"I'll give you all the money in my piggy bank—there's lots—and my marbles, and my desserts for a month, and . . ." She pounded her thighs with her fists. "Pleeease . . ."

"Come on, Evan," Teddy pleaded. "Be a sport."

Evan planted the locket in his breast pocket. "No."

Throckmorton knew that years from now, he would remember the moment when Olivia's locket was opened by the children.

Yes, years from now, Throckmorton would remember thinking: Now that the locket's been opened, it can never be closed.

Annaliese locked her bedroom door, daring for the first time to break one of her father's strictest rules. She pressed her back against it, doubled over, and trapped Throckmorton in a ferocious squeeze underneath her folded arms.

"Why is everything such a deep dark secret?" she blurted, choking on her words. "Why does Evan have to be so mean? Why is Father always so angry? Why won't anybody ever tell me the truth?"

Annaliese's anguished feelings traveled like a fast-moving thunderstorm—shaking shoulders, great gulping sobs, and a brief but violent shower of tears.

And then the squall was over.

She flipped Throckmorton onto her pale pink bedspread, where he landed on his stomach. His head drooped over the ruffled edge, giving him a bird's eye view as she pulled the golden crocodile-leather suitcase out from under her bed.

Annaliese lifted the flat hinged lid and set the stays.

Bailey, who'd followed them out of Evan's bedroom, trotted over and sniffed the suitcase as if it was prey.

Whop!

The agitated bloodhound whacked the bedcovers with his rigid, wagging tail.

Whop!

Throckmorton slithered—*swish!*—into a pool of blue-green silk. A wave of gold fringe splashed in his face.

Much to his surprise he was lying on the same shimmering shawl that Teddy had once held up to the light.

"Oh my gosh!" Annaliese exclaimed, quickly positioning Throckmorton upright inside the lid.

Piece by piece, she held up her discoveries: a garnet-red blouse, a swishy skirt with skinny pleats, a wide leather belt with an ornate buckle, and a pair of lace-up leather boots with worn-down heels. She tried on a flannel hat with a wide brim, stroked the fingers of a deerskin glove, pressed a cotton camisole to her nose and breathed in its scent.

A few of the pieces were stained, others wrinkled or torn. Inside the richly-lined suitcase, the clothing seemed common and out of place.

Annaliese buttoned the wine-colored blouse over her dress. She stepped into the skirt, rolled up the waistband and cinched it with the belt. She slipped on the boots, tightened the laces, and tied them with a double knot.

More so than ever, Annaliese's resemblance to Olivia—the moody eyes, dimples, and driftwood-colored hair—was unmistakable. And yet Throckmorton had never heard anyone—father, aunt, uncle, or cousin—ever say, "Why, Annaliese, you look just like your mother."

Suddenly, Throckmorton's mind flashed back to the day when he'd seen Olivia for the first time.

On the morning of Annaliese's christening, Great-Grandmama Easterling had placed Throckmorton's newly sewn body between layers of crisp tissue paper inside a rectangular white box. The tissue, he recalled, had tickled his nose.

Later, a young woman with deep-set eyes—Olivia—lifted the tissue paper off his face. She fingered his embroidered nose, black button eyes, and smiling red mouth. She pulled a small parchment scroll, tied with a skinny blue cord, out from under his arm.

"Ah, the birth certificate," she said to Great-Grandmama, who stood nearby.

Olivia untied the cord, unrolled the scroll, and read his name aloud: "Throckmorton S. Monkey."

Olivia looked up at Great-Grandmama. "Oh, Ethel, he's wonderful!" she said. "Annaliese will love him; she'll always love him."

Love . . . always. . .

Words that had filled his heart with hope.

From that day forward, Throckmorton assumed his post in Annaliese's hand-carved cradle. Day and night, he kept watch. Whenever Baby Annaliese opened her eyes, he smiled down on her.

After a while, Olivia came to the nursery less and less often. A hired nurse began working around the clock. And then one day, Throckmorton overheard Madge tell the nursemaid that Annaliese's mother was gone for good.

The news devastated Throckmorton. He could still hear the vicious gossip: *Everyone knew the marriage wouldn't work . . . his mother was furious . . . the P sisters fit to be tied . . . a foreigner . . . so young, so poor . . . no one in the family liked her.*

Why *had* the judge married someone so different from himself? Throckmorton couldn't help but wonder.

"Look at this, Throckmorton!" Annaliese now exclaimed.

Abruptly, Throckmorton returned to the present moment.

While he'd been ruminating, she'd dug deeper into the pockets of Olivia's suitcase and pulled out a comb, hairbrush, and silver hand mirror.

Annaliese traced an ornate oval engraved on the mirror's backside. "*O*, for Olivia," she sighed. "Just think—my mother looked into this very same mirror."

Annaliese gazed at the beveled glass with undisguised longing in her eyes. Then, in a hushed and lonely voice, she asked the mirror image:

"Where are you?"

"Why did you leave?"

"Aren't you ever coming back?"

Annaliese's questions were like sharp little arrows stabbing Throckmorton's heart.

From down the hall, Throckmorton now heard the sound of heavy footsteps approaching. Bailey snapped to attention.

Annaliese's bedroom door handle jiggled. "Annaliese, I'm ready to leave for London," called the judge. "I've come to say good-bye."

Uh-oh—now what?

The door rattled in its frame. "Annaliese, are you in there?"

Annaliese pressed the suitcase lid shut.

Throckmorton's limber body bent in half; his lips kissed his knees.

Gadzooks!

He'd been buried alive . . .

Annaliese gave the suitcase a hard shove. Throckmorton felt his satin-lined casket shimmy as it skimmed across the wood floor underneath Annaliese's bed.

The pounding got louder.

"Open this door! Right now! I mean it!"

A few seconds later, Throckmorton heard Judge Easterling's voice strike like a thunderbolt. "Annaliese, where did you get those clothes?"

"They're mine."

"They are NOT yours."

Throckmorton imagined how furious the judge must look—his fisted hands stuffed into the pockets of his trousers, nostrils flaring, lips tightened and hard.

"Annaliese," he said, "I asked you an honest question and I expect an honest answer: Where did you get those clothes?"

"I found them."

"You kids were in the attic, weren't you? You know better than that!" he ranted. "Who let you in?"

Silence.

Throckmorton cringed.

"That's where you found the sock monkeys, isn't it? Did you find anything else?"

"No, Father. I didn't."

"Take them off NOW! They are NOT yours— and I NEVER want to see you wearing them again."

"Yes, Father." Annaliese's voice trembled.

"And no more locking the door!"

Slam!

Lying alone in the sea of Olivia's clothing,

Throckmorton sniffed her once-familiar, long-lingering scent—a strange mixture of talcum powder and wild roses, sweat, cinnamon and salt air.

He asked himself the question he'd asked so many times before: Why, oh why had she left them all behind?

If only he could wriggle out of the jaws of this golden suitcase, he'd crawl into Annaliese's lap and tell her everything he knew about her mother.

How Olivia liked lard sandwiches, pickled herring, and playing the harmonica. Or how she had trained a neighborly albino squirrel to eat apple cores out of her hand.

No more secrets. No more silence.

Soon, the suitcase shifted. The lid lifted, and a shaft of afternoon sunshine slashed across Throckmorton's face.

Annaliese fished him out, holding his body against her stomach as if he, and only he, could stop the pain. Bailey nuzzled up against them. The dog drool moistened Throckmorton's tail, but this time he forgave the old hound.

After a few moments, Madge stormed into Annaliese's bedroom. A sour expression scrunched the maid's ruddy face. "Where's the clothes the mister said you can't wear anymore that's going to the poor?"

Annaliese marched into her closet, yanked an

armful of sweaters off a shelf, and shoved them into Madge's waiting arms.

"These 'ere look brand new," Madge groused.

"Take them, please," Annaliese said in her well-practiced "good girl" voice.

Madge hesitated. Her mouth opened and closed but no words came out.

"Take them!" Annaliese ordered.

"Listen 'ere, Little Miss Rich Girl . . . I heard you bawling in here before—just like when you were a baby . . . a bad baby . . . Waa, waa, waa!" mocked the maid, her thieving hands on her rocking hips. "No wonder your mother . . ."

"Get out! NOW!" Annaliese yelled. "Before I . . ."

Annaliese grabbed her own hairbrush off her dressing table and made out as if she might throw it.

The disgruntled maid scurried off.

"I wish Father would fire that fish-faced old cow!"

Throckmorton seriously doubted that he would. In Judge Easterling's presence—*Presto!*—Madge always changed from churlish to charming.

Annaliese lifted Olivia's hand mirror up to her scowling face. "I'm sick and tired of being a good girl!" she spewed.

She stripped the two rosy-red ribbons off the ends of her perfectly plaited hair and removed the rubber bands. With clawed fingers, she combed the crinkled strands. Then, with one furious shake of her head, she gave her long hair permission to fly free.

Next, she placed a pair of shiny, patent leather shoes in front of Bailey's snout and ordered him to chew.

Yikes, yikes, double-yikes!

Throckmorton had *never* seen Annaliese act like this before . . .

But the angry little girl wasn't finished.

With ragged snips of a sharp shears, she cut— one, two, three, four—sashes off her pretty pastel dresses.

And later, in the library, when no one was watching, she threw the strips of fancy fabric into the fire's flames and patiently watched them burn.

Creeping Secrets

Judge Easterling departed for England without further incident—at least none that Throckmorton knew about.

Mrs. Wiggins rang the dinner bell at precisely six o'clock. Teddy and Annaliese, with Captain Eugene and Throckmorton in hand, reported back to the breakfast nook where the eventful day had commenced.

Annaliese and Teddy placed their sock monkeys side by side on the wooden tabletop. Throckmorton's arm lay comfortably across Captain Eugene's shoulder.

Oh, what a curious day it had been, Throckmorton reflected. . . .

Eastcliff's attic finally unlocked; a door to a hidden room detected; a telltale locket discovered; the lid of a golden crocodile suitcase lifted; anger rising, fists flying, and two seemingly senseless sock monkeys set free.

In the background, a radio announcer described the rising temperatures and strong winds driving sheets of snow and sleet eastward across the frozen sea.

The judge's journey, Throckmorton noted, was probably not getting off to a good start.

Mrs. Wiggins, who usually took Sunday nights off, scurried about the kitchen. She placed a platter of cold sausages, smoked fish, pickles, cheeses, and bread in the center of the wooden table. When the timer went off, she pulled a sheet of molasses cookies out of the oven and filled three glasses with milk.

"Mrs. Wiggins, why don't you go home now?" Annaliese urged. "Don't worry, I'll clean up."

"Why thank you, dear." The cook's shoulders slumped. "I believe that I will." She untied her apron strings and slipped her rosary into her black handbag. "By the way, where's Evan?" she asked. "It's not like him to skip a meal."

"He said he wasn't hungry," Teddy answered.

"That's odd . . . ," Mrs. Wiggins murmured, wedging her feet into her galoshes.

"I think that Evan's pretty upset," Teddy told Annaliese glumly after Mrs. Wiggins left. "But he'd never admit it."

Annaliese pushed her dinner plate off to the side. "I guess I'm not hungry either . . ."

Meticulously, Teddy spread yellow mustard across two pieces of pumpernickel bread. He forked a chunk of liver sausage, stripped off its casing, and cut it into thin slices.

"I saw her once, you know," Teddy said in his most top secret tone of voice.

"Her?" Annaliese whispered, although no one else was in the room. "You mean . . . our mother?"

Teddy nodded.

"Where?"

"Here, at Eastcliff," Teddy answered. "Uh, not exactly here, but sort of."

"When?"

"I'll tell you . . ." Teddy's eyes travelled from one corner of the kitchen to the other. "But you have to promise not to say anything to Evan."

"I promise."

Teddy took a big bite of his sandwich. He chewed slowly, stretching out the impact of his startling revelation.

Annaliese curled herself into the corner of the nook. She pressed her knees against her chest and rubbed at her neck.

"So tell me already."

"It was a couple of years ago, in June," Teddy began. "Father and I'd driven into Bay Fortune. I don't remember why. On our way home, we came around that big curve—you know, the one right before the Murphy farm? An automobile, one I'd never seen before, was parked along the side of the road. It didn't have a Maine license plate.

"A couple hundred yards ahead of us—not far from our mailbox—a woman was walking on our side of the road, close to the ditch. The lupines were in bloom," Teddy noted. "Oh, and she was wearing a hat with a wide brim.

"I didn't get a good look at her. When she heard our car coming, I guess, she bent over—like she was picking flowers.

"Father looked over his shoulder at her as we passed. Then, pow! He stepped on the gas, sped up the lane, roared into the circle, and slammed on the brakes.

"'Get out now,' he told me, 'I forgot something in the village. I'll be right back.'"

Annaliese reached for a piece of bread and started to pull out its soft center. "How did you know who it was, if you didn't see her face?"

"Remember what you told us before, up in Evan's room when you saw her photograph, that you *knew* her? That's what it was like," Teddy explained. "I didn't *see* her, but I knew it *was* her."

Annaliese sat upright. "Did she ever come back?"

"Not that I know of," Teddy answered.

Annaliese wadded the bread into a crumbly lump. She rolled the lump around in her hands and then dropped it on her empty plate. "Let's go look for her—right now!" she said excitedly. "We can find her! I know we can."

"Annaliese, don't be silly," laughed Teddy halfheartedly. "Neither of us can drive. We don't have any money. Not only that, I'm leaving for St. John's Military Academy, right after Great-Grandmama's party."

With a sardonic smile on his face, Teddy saluted.

"Besides," he argued, "she could be anywhere . . ."

"What am I supposed to do here all by myself?" Annaliese's voice rose to a jagged pitch. "Eastcliff's like a prison. Father's always working. No one ever visits . . ."

"Mrs. Wiggins is here," said Teddy. "And Miss Pine—she's pretty nice. And don't forget: Great-Grandmama's birthday party is just around the corner."

Annaliese rubbed her palms up and down her cheeks. Her fingernails were ragged and red around the edges. "Miss Pine will leave," she said. "Just like all the rest."

She pulled Throckmorton into her arms and gave him a desperate hug.

I won't leave . . .

Throckmorton silently assured her.

I promise . . .

Until death—my untimely demise, or Madge's next dirty trick—do us part.

Yet, deep in his heart, Throckmorton knew that there was one person who'd never abandoned Annaliese.

Day in and day out, her father went to work early in the morning and came home late at night, but he always came home. To Throckmorton's knowledge, tonight was the first night he'd spent away from Eastcliff since . . . well, since Olivia left.

Judge Easterling, for better or worse, had never deserted his post.

Even Throckmorton—hardly the judge's biggest fan—gave him credit for that.

Teddy washed down his sandwich and a handful of cookies with a glass of milk. "Annaliese, someday we *will* go looking for her," he promised, rising to his feet. "Somehow, we'll figure out a way to find her—but we'll have to wait until we're older and Father can't stand in our way."

Annaliese crossed her arms on the table and put her head down. Throckmorton was about to slide off her lap, when she reached out her hand to prevent his fall.

Annaliese straightened her back and used Throckmorton's soft and willing hand to wipe a splash of salty teardrops off her cheeks.

"Teddy, please," she begged, "tell Father that you don't want to go to that horrid academy . . . Evan can go—he'll do fine without you."

"Annaliese, listen up." Teddy paused. His countenance grew more mature by the minute. "If Mother came back once," he said, "she'll come back again. And one of us has to be here at Eastcliff when she does."

Throckmorton completely understood what Teddy was asking his sister to do:

Be a good soldier . . .

Smile . . .

Hold down the fort . . .

However, Annaliese was neither a soldier nor a hand-stitched sock monkey. Throckmorton's sweet and very sad keeper was a young girl who yearned for the kind of love she'd never had.

Rats, rats, triple-rats!

Why did life have to be so atrociously unfair?

Now Throckmorton heard Teddy take the first step up the servants' staircase.

"Hey, Teddy," Annaliese called out.

"Yeah?" he answered.

"Thanks for telling me."

Glumly, Annaliese put together a plate of food for Evan. She refrigerated the leftovers, washed the dishes, and put them in the drainer to dry, softly singing:

Sock monkey, Throck-monkey, needle-in-a-haystack monkey . . .

Annaliese traipsed up the stairs with Evan's supper in one hand and Throckmorton hanging in the other, still singing.

As he listened to the words of Annaliese's nonsensical songs, Throckmorton couldn't help but wonder: How many more secrets are still creeping inside Eastcliff's crumbling walls?

In the days that followed, Annaliese tended the things that Olivia left behind as though they were orphaned children.

She unpacked and packed the suitcase, unfolded and refolded the clothes. She zipped zippers, buttoned buttons, snapped snaps, and hooked eyes. She washed the clothes that were dirty, mended the torn, and ironed the wrinkled.

Every morning she brushed out her hair with Olivia's brush. Soon Annaliese's lighter strands comingled with her mother's darker strands still stuck in the bristles.

Every night before she went to bed, she wrapped the shimmering shawl around her shoulders, as if the shawl were love.

Watching these sweet, sad rituals tore at Throckmorton's heart.

One afternoon, she lifted an ivory satin gown with lace sleeves out of the dress box. The hem was soiled, and a large section of the long skirt had been snipped out.

"Look, Throckmorton. I noticed this the other day—it's ruined."

Later she asked Miss Pine if she could have the little wedding dress that Miss Beatrice had been wearing, but Miss Pine said no.

Annaliese waited a few hours and then asked again.

"When your father comes home, ask him if you can have the dress," Miss Pine responded. "It's not mine to give away."

As the days passed, Annaliese grew quieter and withdrew deeper and deeper into herself. Evan and Teddy, Miss Pine told her, were busy studying for the placement tests that they'd have to take at their new school. Throckmorton spent most daylight hours lolling around a lamp, which was fashioned into a wishing well, on Annaliese's nightstand.

One morning when Throckmorton woke, he felt unusually flat and cranky. All night long he'd been pinned beneath Annaliese's restless body while she tossed about like a boat in waves of bad dreams.

When she got up, her hair was a tangled, mangled mess. On top of her twisted sheet, Throckmorton lay patiently, hoping and praying that she'd fluff up his stuffing before she went downstairs.

He heard a gentle rap on the door.

Probably Miss Pine.

Miss Pine, he'd noticed, had sensed Annaliese's distress over the last few days and decided to let her be.

Throckmorton's opinion of the new nanny had risen considerably.

"Annaliese!" the nanny called softly.

"What?" Annaliese called back.

"Great-Grandmama Easterling just phoned up. She wants to see you and Throckmorton. We'll eat a quick breakfast and then be on our way."

"She does?" Annaliese drew open the door. "Why?"

"Just hurry up and get dressed. The walk will do you good."

Hooray for today!

He was off to see his maker!

Throckmorton felt puffier and fluffier already.

He, Annaliese, and Miss Pine followed a half-mile long footpath through a stand of crystallized pines, over an icy footbridge, and past the frozen river where Evan and Teddy played hockey with chums on Saturday nights.

About a year earlier, Ethel Constance Easterling announced that she'd grown weary of her great wealth; she preferred the company of Clydesdales to circles of high society.

The family's matriarch had moved from Boston's Beacon Hill neighborhood back to the Easterling estate. She remodeled the second story of Eastcliff's carriage house into living quarters. She'd moved into the lofty space above the stable the previous spring. Never, she claimed, had she been happier.

"Are you and your great-grandmother close?" asked Miss Pine as the path narrowed. "I mean, do you visit her often?"

"Evan and Teddy and I did, a few times, when she first moved back—then on Thanksgiving and Christmas Eve, too, I guess. I've tried to visit her again, but every time I ask, Father comes up with a reason why I can't. He says that Great-Grandmama puts crazy ideas in my head."

"Like what?" Miss Pine asked.

"Like birthday parties—Father doesn't believe in them."

"He doesn't? Not at all?"

"Not the kind with kids and pony rides and party favors, like our cousins have. Father says that we get plenty of presents, we don't need a party besides."

"So, how do you and your brothers celebrate your birthdays?"

"Mrs. Wiggins always asks us ahead of time what we want to eat for dinner, and whatever we ask for, she'll make," Annaliese answered. "For my last birthday—my worst birthday—I ordered . . ."

Annaliese stopped herself.

"Your worst birthday?" Miss Pine questioned. "Why?"

"Everyone forgot, and I ate by myself."

"Oh my," said Miss Pine, "that's awful."

Throckmorton remembered Annaliese's ninth birthday—on May 23rd—vividly, as if it were yesterday.

It was worse than awful . . .

First, the judge called from the courthouse to say that he had a hung jury; he didn't know when he'd be home. Evan and Teddy went horseback riding with the Murphy boys and lost track of time. Uncle Ray and Aunt Pansy had car trouble, and Great-Grandmama, whom Annaliese had invited, came down with a cold.

Annaliese and Miss Pine walked in silence to the top of a small ridge. On the far side of a broad meadow robed in new snow, Great-Grandmama's carriage house came into view.

"I can see how . . . ," Miss Pine started to say, lightly touching Annaliese's shoulder.

Annaliese shook off Miss Pine's touch and broke into a run. "What I want to see are the horses!" she cried.

When they reached the ground-floor stable, Annaliese jingled a leather strap of sleigh bells hanging next to the rolling door.

Throckmorton was so excited his eyelashes tingled. Over the years, he'd seen Great-Grandmama only a few times. In his mind, she was tall and strong, smart and kind. She dressed in long flowing skirts and had deft fingers weighed down by expensive rings—diamonds, emeralds, sapphires, rubies.

Once, when he was eavesdropping, he'd heard Mrs. Wiggins say that Great-Grandmama had a mild form of a debilitating disease. Still, Throckmorton was shocked when he saw her.

The silver-haired woman who greeted them stood barely as tall as Annaliese. She wore a short black belted dress with a white collar and pearl buttons. A lacy handkerchief peeked out of her breast pocket.

On her left leg, beneath her knee, an iron brace was attached to a high-topped, lace-up shoe. The silver handle of her cane was fashioned into the head of a fox. She wore only one ring: a diamond as big as Bailey's nose, brilliant as sunshine on fresh snow.

"Come in, come in," Great-Grandmama urged, waving her cane. "Bring some of that lovely snow with you!"

Great-Grandmama placed her trembling fingertips on Throckmorton's cheek, like a blessing. "It's good to see you again, Throckmorton."

"And you, too," she told Annaliese. "I've told my horses that you were coming. They're very excited."

Throckmorton was taken aback. He'd never considered the possibility that a horse or dog or creature of any kind might have feelings as real as a red-heeled sock monkey's.

Once inside, a slight grizzled man stepped forward. Max Wiggins, stable keeper and husband of Eastcliff's cook, was a former jockey and jack-of-all-trades.

"Are you from around these parts?" he asked Miss Pine once they were introduced.

"No, I'm not," she answered. "I'm a city girl. Born and raised in South Boston."

The horse stable, Throckmorton couldn't help but notice, was almost as elegant as Eastcliff itself—heated, draped, and rich with the odor of hay, manure, leather, and horse flesh.

Horse tack—saddles, collars, reins—hung on the mahogany walls, its leather polished to a rich luster, brass hardware gleaming. Ribbons—blue, and purple grand champion, trimmed with gold—decorated the window frames. Over the years, in Great-Grandmama's absence, Max had showed the draft horses in competitions as if they were his own.

Great-Grandmama led them down the aisle, four stalls on each side. The Clydesdales had long black tails and silken manes. Beautifully groomed feathering hung from their knees to their hooves.

The monumental size of the horses stunned Throckmorton. Even the tall Miss Pine was dwarfed in their presence. He chuckled inside, thinking about how big his smile would be if he were the size of a Clydesdale.

"Magnificent, aren't they?" asked Great-Grandmama, beaming like a proud parent. Fearlessly, she stroked a horse's flank. "This boy here, Prince Daniel, he's sixteen hands."

"Weighs almost a ton," Max added.

Max helped Annaliese mount a bench that ran along the side of Prince Daniel's stall.

"Look, Throckmorton," she said, stroking the white blaze on his bay face. "Isn't he beautiful?"

The horse responded with a hay-scented snort.

"Aye, Missy, they are noble beasts," said Max. "Best friends a man—or a woman—could have. And soon to be put to work, I hear."

"Why's that?" Miss Pine asked.

"For my birthday party," Great-Grandmama answered. "Four teams of two, pulling scarlet-and-cream sleighs. They'll bring folks from the main road, up the lane to the manor house."

"Can you imagine . . . ," Miss Pine said.

"Speaking of the party . . . ," said Great-Grandmama. "Let's go upstairs, shall we? I'd like to tell you why I invited you here."

In Great-Grandmama's light-filled quarters, tall arched windows faced the frozen, crystal-bright sea. Eastcliff's hallways bore portraits of grim ancestors in gold frames. Here, sepia-toned photos of Great-Grandmama's prizewinning horses adorned the walls.

"Sit down, sit down," Great-Grandmama urged. "I set out some scones. Please help yourself to tea."

Miss Pine and Annaliese hung their coats on a mirrored hall tree. They took seats in wing chairs next to side tables crowded with framed photos of red-heeled sock monkeys.

"Ma'am, I'm curious," said Miss Pine after they'd spent a few minutes exchanging pleasantries, "about your sock monkeys."

"Why I made them? Is that what you're asking?" Miss Pine nodded.

"When I was a child, about Annaliese's age, my sock puppet—that's what we called them back then—helped me through many a tough moment."

"What was his name?" Annaliese asked.

"Mr. Puddles."

"Do you still have him?"

"No, my dear, I do not. But I've never forgotten him. Even when all that was left of him was a couple of buttons and a scrap of sock, Mr. Puddles was my favorite toy."

Great-Grandmama rose from the settee where she'd been sitting and walked across the high-ceilinged room. She motioned for Miss Pine, Annaliese, and Throckmorton to join her in front of the fireplace. "There's something I'd like to show you."

A huge painting hung above the fireplace mantel. An intricate rendering of a majestic gold- and green-leafed tree was framed behind glass.

Annaliese stood on her tiptoes and squinted at lines of fine print written on the tree's leaves and branches. "Macarthur S. Monkey, Fairfax S. Monkey, Daisy S. Monkey," she read. "Why, it's the sock monkeys' family tree!"

Miss Pine took a closer look. "The painting is lovely."

"My oldest son, George, who lives on Long Island, commissioned the work in honor of my upcoming birthday. He hung it here on Christmas Day."

Annaliese held Throckmorton up and pressed his hand on a line of letters and numbers. "There you are! 'Throckmorton S. Monkey.' Your birthdate is the same as mine."

"I've made forty-nine sock monkeys," Great-Grandmama told them, "for forty-nine babies born into the Easterling family."

She lifted a leather-bound ledger lying open on an end table. "I keep a written record of my sock monkeys in here: names, keepers' names, birthdates, descriptions of their features, the outfits that I've made them . . . that sort of thing."

Annaliese's eyes widened with surprise. "Forty-nine sock monkeys and their keepers are invited to your birthday party?"

"Exactly."

Throckmorton was flabbergasted. He never realized that he had *that* many sock monkey cousins.

"Did Throckmorton come with a costume?" Annaliese asked sheepishly. "Or did I lose it?"

"No, he didn't."

Throckmorton sighed. One of his great sorrows was that Great-Grandmama hadn't made him a stylish suit of clothes. He didn't know why. The question had haunted him all of his life.

Great-Grandmama flipped to a different page in the ledger. "See? Next to Throckmorton's name, I've written 'Natural.'"

Natural?

As far as Throckmorton was concerned, she may as well have written *Boring, uninteresting, and easily forgotten.*

"Throckmorton is the last sock monkey I made," Great-Grandmama explained. "By then I'd started to appreciate the simpler things in life." She settled herself back onto the settee. "However, with Mr. Puddles long gone, I have no sock monkey of my own."

Great-Grandmama's eyes twinkled mischievously. "And if *I* have no sock monkey, who will take *me* to *my* party?"

"But you're the birthday girl!" Annaliese exclaimed.

"That, my dear, is precisely the reason why you're here."

"I don't understand."

"You, young lady, are going to make a sock monkey for me."

"Me? I don't know how to make a sock monkey. I mean, I know how to sew a little bit, but—why don't you make one yourself?"

Great-Grandmama lifted her small wrinkled right hand. Her fingers were fluttering, and she couldn't make them stop.

"Can you thread a needle?" she asked Annaliese. "Can you cut with scissors?"

Annaliese nodded.

Meanwhile Throckmorton, by nature observant and sensitive to the feelings of others, had noticed that something was bothering Miss Pine.

He couldn't imagine what.

While Annaliese and Great-Grandmama discussed the construction of sock monkeys, Miss Pine paced back and forth between the horse photos on the wall, the leather ledger, and the sock monkey family tree.

"Mrs. Easterling, do you have any pictures of Annaliese and their brothers when they were babies?" she now asked. "I haven't seen any at Eastcliff. I was hoping that you might."

"Why, no, I don't believe I do," Great-Grandmama replied. She handed Annaliese a pair of red-heeled wool socks. "Let's get started, shall we?"

Miss Pine appeared agitated and in a hurry to leave. "I'm not sure that today will work out," she said with a forced smiled. "Thank you, Mrs. Easterling, but we really must be going."

Now, everyone knew that Great-Grandmama Easterling was used to playing by her own rules.

"But I thought . . . certainly you can . . . ," she sputtered.

Miss Pine lifted Annaliese's coat off the hall tree. "Come along now, Annaliese."

"It's not even ten o'clock," Great-Grandmama argued. "We have all day."

"I don't want to go back to Eastcliff," Annaliese whined. "We just got here!"

Miss Pine wouldn't budge. "I've scheduled Evan

and Teddy for their Latin lessons later this morning. Annaliese studies French. And this afternoon, all three have reading and composition." She paused. "Tomorrow, perhaps."

Great-Grandmama pursed her lips, but pressed no further.

Seeing her great-grandmother's crest-fallen face, Annaliese made a suggestion. "Maybe I—I mean, Throckmorton—could stay here with you overnight."

A jolly good idea!

A pajama party *sans* pajamas.

Great-Grandmama forced a smile. "Why yes, I'd like that very much."

Annaliese pressed Throckmorton into his maker's shaky hands.

Great-Grandmama's eyes, as sharp and cold as icicles, narrowed.

"Miss Pine, I expect to see Annaliese on my doorstep tomorrow morning at nine o'clock on the dot. I'll accept no more excuses."

"Until tomorrow, then . . ."

And just like that, Miss Pine bundled Annaliese up and hustled her out Great-Grandmama's door.

An Uninvited Guest

Great-Grandmama wasted no time sharing her soured opinion of Miss Pine with Throckmorton.

"Why, I never . . . ," she spouted, pacing between pieces of furniture. "Who does she think she is?"

Great-Grandmama tossed aside her cane, leaned against a round claw-foot table in the center of the room, and wrung her hands.

"She's just lucky that I shipped Ellis off to London or I'd send that young so-and-so packing too. Otherwise there'd be no one to watch the children at night."

Off and on for the next few hours, Great-Grandmama stewed and fumed. Throckmorton—who considered Miss Pine quite plucky and plenty fine—had a hard time listening to her complaints. Fortunately, Great-Grandmama sipped a cordial with her afternoon tea and then promptly fell asleep on the settee.

Throckmorton, who lay by her side, stirred when he heard the sound of footsteps on the outside staircase.

"That's probably my supper," said Great-Grandmama, yawning as she woke. "Mrs. Wiggins prepares a hot meal for me each evening, which Max delivers."

After a tap or two, it was not Max but Miss Pine who stepped into Great-Grandmama's quarters.

A blast of bitterly cold air swept into the room.

"Please forgive the intrusion, Mrs. Easterling," she said, closing the door, "but I really must speak with you."

Great-Grandmama's crocheted shawl slipped off her shoulders as she took Throckmorton up into her lap. "Please come in, Miss Pine," she said, "since it seems you're going to, whether you've been invited or not."

Miss Pine got right down to business.

"Mrs. Easterling, I'm here to discuss Annaliese." She removed her black leather gloves, twisting the pair as she spoke. "I know that I've only been here a short time, but I'm very concerned about her."

Great-Grandmama lifted her chin and looked off to the side. "The child seems perfectly fine to me."

"Appearances, I've learned, can be deceiving," said Miss Pine, "especially when it comes to children. I regret to say that Annaliese is a very unhappy young girl and probably has been for a long time."

Throckmorton felt Great-Grandmama's body stiffen. "Whatever are you talking about?" she demanded. "This morning Annaliese was all smiles—until you dragged her away."

"A sock monkey smiles all the time as well. However, in Annaliese's case . . ."

Great-Grandmama frowned. "Miss Pine, my guiding light has been to keep my nose out of other people's affairs. Stick to my own business."

"I assumed your great-granddaughter was your business," said Miss Pine. "And if she's not, perhaps she should be."

Holy mackerel!

Throckmorton had never heard *anyone* talk to Great-Grandmama so, so . . . bluntly.

If they did, she'd cut them out of her will for sure!

"Miss Pine, Annaliese is my grandson's business. And Ellis has made it perfectly clear that I am not to meddle in his children's lives." Great-Grandmama threw up her bony, quivering hands. "And why you think she's unhappy is beyond me."

"Annaliese has no friends," Miss Pine calmly explained. "She's not permitted to go to school. She's an exceptionally intelligent child—yet, in spite of years of private tutoring, way behind in her lessons." Miss Pine paused, as if to weigh her next words. "And somewhere out there she has a mother whom she is not allowed to speak about, much less see."

"Olivia left," Great-Grandmama said in a contemptuous tone of voice, "of her own free will."

Miss Pine leaned forward. "And she *never once* tried to come back? *Never once* wrote her children? *Never once* phoned them up?"

"Like I said before, Miss Pine, I've learned to stick to my own business."

Miss Pine abruptly stood, marched over to the fireplace, and glared at the sock monkey family tree.

"The night before last," said Miss Pine, "I found Annaliese in Judge Easterling's study, where he spends most of his time when he is home. His study, by the way, is strictly off-limits to the children. Annaliese was staring at a page in the middle of a big thick book. When she saw me coming, she slammed the book shut."

"And?" asked Great-Grandmama.

"She was looking at the family Bible. A black ribbon bookmarked the page. Inside, as you must know, are pages and pages of family history—names, places of birth, dates of death—the Easterling family tree, going back hundreds of years.

"Above Annaliese and her brothers' names was a bracket leading to their father's name; but next to it, where Olivia's name should be, the information was clipped out."

"Miss Pine, what are you trying to say?"

"How can Annaliese—or Evan or Teddy, for that matter—grow up with a strong sense of who they are and where they come from when everyone pretends that their mother never existed? Why, it's as if Annaliese were to stand in front of a full-length mirror and see only one half of her body reflected!"

"Miss Pine, as much as I appreciate your opinions—and your metaphor, by the way—I must warn you . . ."

In the midst of such a heated argument, Throckmorton felt silly, sitting there with a smile on his face. Like most red-heeled sock monkeys, he'd often wished that the way he looked on the outside matched the way he felt on the inside.

"Children know when they're being deceived." Miss Pine's voice grew louder and more agitated. "They want the truth. And sooner or later, they'll find a way to dig it up."

"And you've had personal experience with such matters, Miss Pine?" Great-Grandmama said.

A scarlet flush colored the nanny's face.

"Let me tell you something," said Great-Grandmama sternly. "Olivia broke my grandson's heart and wounded his pride. You see, Miss Pine, we Easterlings don't divorce. Our spouses die and then, as they say, life goes on."

"So Judge Easterling and Olivia *are* divorced?" Miss Pine asked. "Do their children know that?"

"I'll see you out." Great-Grandmama gripped the silver handle of her cane and rose to her feet.

Throckmorton toppled onto his side.

"Please, Mrs. Easterling, try to understand . . ." Miss Pine breathed in deeply. "Certainly you can find a way to show a lonely little girl that you care as much about her as you do your horses and . . ." With one finger, Miss Pine hooked Throckmorton's ear, stringing him up like a fish. "Your stuffed socks."

Stuffed sock???

Miss Pine's affront to the sock monkey species pierced *his* heart and hurt *his* pride. And yet, deep down, he knew that Miss Pine spoke the truth about Annaliese.

For years, Throckmorton had wanted to believe that Annaliese was as happy as any child without a mother could be.

But he was wrong: Annaliese wasn't happy.

Any sock monkey who'd watched her unpack her missing mother's suitcase, dozens and dozens of times, would draw the same conclusion.

"Miss Pine, I've heard quite enough. And let me remind you, jobs these days are . . ."

Miss Pine let Throckmorton's limp body drop back onto the settee.

"Earlier this week," the nanny said, "I gave the children a writing assignment. They were to describe something that they were very proud of doing, or something that they regret."

Miss Pine pulled some sheets of paper out of her handbag and laid them on top of Great-Grandmama's ledger. "I think you'll find that Annaliese's words speak for themselves. Good night, Mrs. Easterling." Miss Pine closed the door behind her.

Great-Grandmama stood stiffly, gripping the back of the settee, taking a series of shorter and shorter breaths. For a second or two, she seemed to Throckmorton to be not breathing at all.

Finally (*thank heavens!*) she sharply exhaled through her teeth, released her cane, and eased her shaking body onto the cushions, where she covered herself and Throckmorton with the crocheted shawl.

For a long time, Great-Grandmama's fingertips tapped ceaselessly on Throckmorton's back. He pictured her anxious thoughts stampeding like stallions across her troubled mind.

Great-Grandmama never did eat the hot supper that Max Wiggins delivered shortly after Miss Pine departed. When Max asked Great-Grandmama if she would be coming down to say good night to the Clydesdales, as was her practice, she shook her head no.

She laid Throckmorton next to her pillow and crawled into bed without changing into a nightgown.

The frigid winter night crept on and on toward morning. Shortly before dawn, Great-Grandmama, who'd been unable to sleep, lit a candle set in a pewter candlestick on her bedside table.

She reached for the sheets of paper that Miss Pine left behind and, in the flame's flickering yellow light, read Annaliese's words in complete silence.

Oh, how Throckmorton longed to hear what Annaliese had written.

Oh, how he longed for the ability to decipher the meaning of the tiny, mystifying symbols that she'd printed.

A few minutes later, Great-Grandmama set the precious pages in her lap. She blew out a breath of air. Their eyes met.

"Oh, all right," she said tenderly. "It is, after all, about you too."

And then, for his (unbecoming) ears only, Great-Grandmama reread Annaliese's words aloud—slowly, with expression—just the way he liked them.

How Throckmorton Got Trapped
in Madge's Smelly Net
The Story of My 9th Birthday
By
Annaliese Elizabeth Easterling

Nothing ever happens at Eastcliff. No one ever comes to visit. Father has had fallings-out with my great-grandmother, most of my aunties and uncles, and just about everybody else. I used to get to play with my cousins once in a while, but not anymore.

Last Saturday, something did happen. The doorbell rang. When I opened the front door, a man in a gray uniform asked to see the lady of the house.

Miss Pine signed for the four letters that he delivered. One of the envelopes was addressed to Mr. Throckmorton S. Monkey. Throckmorton is my sock monkey. I hadn't played with him for a long, long time.

Why not?

It was all because of my ninth birthday (my worst birthday) on May 23rd.

Like I do every year, I asked Mrs. Wiggins to make smoked ham, Boston baked beans, carrot pennies, and angel food cake with fluffy frosting for my birthday dinner.

My old nanny, Miss O'Neil, put a French braid in my hair and tied a bright blue bow on its tail. Blue is my favorite color.

Mrs. Wiggins rang the dinner bell at six o'clock sharp. When I got to the dining room, no one else was there.

Father, Evan, Teddy, Uncle Ray, Aunt Pansy, and Great-Grandmama were supposed to come.

Poor Mrs. Wiggins . . . when I think about it, she did try SO HARD to make it up to me.

She brought Throckmorton; Emma, my china head doll; Romeo, my stuffed pinto pony; and Toady, my favorite brown bear, into the dining room. She set them in the empty chairs like they were party guests. She poured pretend tea into their cups and put tiny pieces of food on their plates. For the first time ever, she took off her apron and took Father's place at the table.

I ate a small plate of food because Mrs. Wiggins had done her best. After she lit the candles and sang the Happy Birthday song, I didn't try to blow the candles out.

Why should I?

My birthday wishes never come true.

Every year I wish that my mother will come back home. But she never does.

After dinner, I dropped Throckmorton and Emma

and Romeo and Toady into a heap on the soft chair in my room. I put on my pajamas and went to bed before the sun even went down.

Later, Evan and Teddy knocked on my bedroom door. I didn't open it. They yelled, "We're sorry!" and went away.

Father came in later, but I threw the covers over my head and pretended that I was asleep. He left a birthday present on the foot of my bed. A diary, exactly like the one he gave me the year before.

After my birthday, I let my bedroom get really, really

messy. That made Madge really, really mad.

One day after lessons, I walked into my bedroom. It was as neat as a pin. My dolls were lined up on the shelves. My other toys were packed away in trunks in my closet. My favorite stuffed animals were strung up in a stinky fishing net high above my bed.

Madge had a wicked smile on her face. She cackled like a witch. "The next time I find one of them toys of yours on the floor, I'll toss it into the sea!"

So, that's when I decided that I was going to grow up as fast as I could. I'd leave home—just like my mother did—and go look for her.

I pretended that I was a famous actress on the deck of a ship. I waved and blew kisses to all my old friends. "Good-bye! Good-bye! I'm growing up," I called. "Be well!"

Not a single one waved back.

After that I stopped playing with toys. Talking to toys is only me talking to myself. Dolls don't listen. Stuffed animals can't sing the Happy Birthday song.

But then when Throckmorton's invitation to Great-Grandmama's ninetieth-birthday party arrived, I felt very, very bad.

I asked Throckmorton to forgive me, and thankfully he did.

The End

As Great-Grandmama uttered the final words of Annaliese's sorrowful story, Throckmorton's eyes burned as if real tears welled up in them.

At the same time, he experienced an overwhelming sense of relief, knowing the reason why Annaliese had abandoned him and that he'd done nothing to deserve such hurtful punishment.

Now, Great-Grandmama stared at Throckmorton's diaper pin as if seeing the little yellow duck for the first time.

The burning wick struggled to stay lit. Soon its golden flame sputtered, spat, and fizzled out.

"Ah, life . . . it is a strange beast," Great-Grandmama murmured as she drifted off to sleep. "And my own, perhaps the strangest of them all."

A Surprise Inside

At precisely nine o'clock the next morning, Miss Pine strode into Great-Grandmama's living quarters with her head held high. Annaliese, who followed behind, was dressed in a tattersall plaid coat, wooly tam, and her favorite pair of bright blue mittens. On her feet, she wore Olivia's lace-up leather boots and two pairs of thick wool socks.

Great-Grandmama smiled and pecked both of Annaliese's cheeks, rosy from the cold. "It's good to see you again." She laid her hands on Annaliese's shoulders. "Why, the older you get," she said softly, "the more you look like your mother."

Annaliese's head jerked back. "Father forbids anyone to talk about my mother."

"Your father's a fool." Great-Grandmama looked up and met Miss Pine's eyes. "Perhaps we all are."

If Miss Pine was shocked by Great-Grandmama's sudden about-face, she didn't show it. Throckmorton wasn't surprised in the least. Everyone knew that Ethel Constance Easterling was every bit as unpredictable as New England's weather.

Miss Pine unwound her scarf and unbuttoned the top button of her coat.

"Thank you, Miss Pine, but Annaliese and I won't require your services," Great-Grandmama said. "However, you may join us at three for afternoon tea."

"And then may I visit the horses again?" Annaliese asked.

Great-Grandmama answered, "Of course."

"Mrs. Wiggins said that a big storm's brewing," Miss Pine explained. "I'll keep my eyes on the weather."

Annaliese picked up Throckmorton, lifted his arm, and made it wave. "See you later!"

Miss Pine offered her hand to Great-Grandmama. "Thank you, Mrs. Easterling."

"Thank you, Miss Pine."

The nanny waved back at Throckmorton, smiled, and took her leave.

"Well then," Great-Grandmama said to Annaliese. "Let's get down to business."

She pointed at the claw-foot table spread with red-heeled work socks, stuffing, scraps of felt and strands of yarn, embroidery thread, buttons, ribbons, and bows.

"Everything's laid out for you."

Annaliese propped Throckmorton against a wicker sewing basket filled with spools of thread, stick pins, needles, sewing shears, and a measuring tape.

Surveying the raw materials, Throckmorton wondered: How had Great-Grandmama transformed such insignificant stuff into sock monkeys who can see, smell, hear, think, and feel?

Annaliese followed Great-Grandmama's directions exactly, but making a red-heeled sock monkey by hand was harder than it looked.

Annaliese turned the red-heeled sock inside out and sewed the seams with uneven stitches.

"Make your stitches smaller," Great-Grandmama told her, "so the stuffing won't come out."

While trimming a seam, Annaliese accidentally cut the thread.

"Everyone makes mistakes, especially the first time," said Great-Grandmama kindly. "Pull out the threads and stitch it again."

Annaliese filled the head, body, and legs with soft stuffing. With her small steady hands she packed the stuffing tight.

Great-Grandmama beamed. "Well done, my dear!"

After lunch, Annaliese was about to sew the sock monkey's stuffed left arm to its body, when Great-Grandmama instructed her to stop.

"But why?" Annaliese asked. "It will leave a hole."

"Sewing on the left arm is the last step. You'll see why in a little while."

For the monkey's smile, Annaliese used a black running stitch across the middle of its red lips. For the tail, she tapered a strip of leftover sock.

"I want my monkey to have button eyes," said Great-Grandmama, "and an embroidered nose."

"Like Throckmorton's? With pretzel-shaped ears?"

"Absolutely," Great-Grandmama chuckled. "They make a monkey easier to hang on to."

Easier to hang on to?

Throckmorton thought that pretzel-shaped ears made a sock monkey look immature and stupid.

For the next few hours, creating the new sock monkey absorbed all of Annaliese's attention. As the loft darkened, Great-Grandmama turned on a few lights. Occasionally, she nodded off to sleep while sitting up in her chair.

"Look, Great-Grandmama!" said Annaliese, nudging her arm. "I'm almost finished."

The new sock monkey turned out to be about the same shape and size as Throckmorton and almost as homely as Miss Beatrice.

Annaliese's uneven stitching made its smile look twisted. The eyebrows were lopsided and the ears didn't match.

"And now the heart," said Great-Grandmama. She pointed at a heart-shaped cookie cutter. "Use the red felt. You'll need two pieces."

"Sock monkeys have hearts?" asked Annaliese.

"*My* sock monkeys have hearts." Great-Grandmama dropped her voice. "With little surprises inside."

"Like Cracker Jacks?"

Great-Grandmama smiled mysteriously. "You might say that."

What did she mean? Throckmorton asked himself. Did he have a surprise inside his heart? If so, what might it be?

His imagination took flight. A cat's-eye marble? A tiny key? A rare coin? A gold doubloon?

Annaliese continued to concentrate on the task at hand. She traced two heart-shaped pieces and cut them to size.

"Pin first and then sew the halves together. Leave an opening on top," Great-Grandmama instructed. "Use your smallest stitch."

The result was a red heart-shaped pocket.

Great-Grandmama wriggled the diamond ring off her finger. "Now, put this ring inside the heart."

"But . . . but . . . ," Annaliese protested, "it's a diamond worth a million gazillion dollars and . . . and . . ."

"Pshaw! A two-hundred-year-old piece of pirate's booty tainted with the blood of evil men,"

Great-Grandmama replied. "A jewel that should be put to good use."

Biting down hard on her lips, Annaliese slipped the diamond ring between the two halves of the felt heart.

"Now, hemstitch the top edges so that the ring doesn't fall out. Once you're finished, put the heart inside the monkey's chest where it belongs."

Annaliese hesitated.

Throckmorton didn't understand what was holding her back.

Great-Grandmama glanced at her watch. "Do as you're told, child," she urged. "We're running out of time."

Between Annaliese's fingers, the red felt heart trembled. Perspiration moistened her forehead. Throckmorton feared that she was about to faint.

"Without a heart," said Great-Grandmama kindly, "a sock monkey is just—it's just a toy."

Annaliese took a deep breath and then pressed the diamond-filled heart into the stuffing. She used an overstitch to stitch the left arm to the armpit.

"Now tell me," said Great-Grandmama after the

heart had found its home. "Is it a boy or a girl? And what's the monkey's name?"

Annaliese dropped her head into her hands. "I don't know . . . I don't know . . ."

"Yes you do. You're the sock monkey's maker." Great-Grandmama laid her hand on top of Annaliese's. "Be still. The sock monkey will reveal its secrets, if you're willing to listen."

Gently, Annaliese tilted her head and then rested her cheek on the sock monkey's chest.

The silence was as loud as a thousand angels praying.

"It's a boy," she said reverently. "His name is Ebenezer. He's a lighthouse keeper."

Ebenezer . . . a handsome name . . . Throckmorton was eager to make his acquaintance.

Suddenly from the floor below, the horses whinnied. Great-Grandmama rushed her next words. "Annaliese, I have one final request. It's a secret. Can you keep a secret?"

Annaliese nodded.

"Someday, I want you to give Ebenezer the Lighthouse Keeper to your mother."

Good galoshes!

Did Throckmorton really just hear what he thought he heard?

Annaliese shook her head, blinking her eyes over

and over as if she'd suddenly lost sight. "But I don't even . . ."

Hurried footsteps now sounded on the stairs outside.

"We treated her badly," Great-Grandmama said in a hushed tone of voice. "It wasn't Olivia's fault, I suppose, that she was so . . . so *different* . . . I should have reined the family in. I've never forgiven myself."

The color drained from Annaliese's confused face. "I don't understand . . ."

"Someday you will. In fact, someday I'll tell you the whole story. But for now, promise me."

"I—I—I promise."

After a few sharp taps on the door, Miss Pine burst into Great-Grandmama's quarters.

"Annaliese!" she cried. "Put on your coat. The snow's coming down in buckets. Hurry—or we'll lose the path!"

"Go with Miss Pine," Great-Grandmama told Annaliese. "And don't worry about a thing . . . we'll talk again soon." Great-Grandmama smiled into Ebenezer's face, and the sock monkey smiled back. "And thank you for making me a sock monkey. He's everything I hoped he would be."

Reluctantly, Annaliese shrugged on her coat. Her blue-green eyes had faded to a grayish, troubled color.

"And Miss Pine, please keep an eye on the child," said Great-Grandmama. "She seems a bit feverish."

Miss Pine pressed her hand on Annaliese's forehead. "Hmm . . . you're right. She's excited about the party, I imagine, and now with her father off to London . . . I'll see that she takes to her bed as soon as we get back to Eastcliff."

Stormy Weather

Beneath her fuzzy tam, Annaliese's face was pallid. Was she sick, Throckmorton wondered, or just bewildered by the secret that Great-Grandmama had asked her to keep?

So many questions without any answers . . .

Did Great-Grandmama know where Olivia went and why she never came back? Did she know where Olivia was now?

If so, why wouldn't Great-Grandmama approach Olivia herself?

If not, how would Annaliese ever find her to give her Ebenezer?

And the most pressing question of all: If the Easterling family had treated Olivia badly, did Great-Grandmama *really* think that she could buy forgiveness with a shiny rock?

Humans were so mysterious. Throckmorton didn't think he'd understand them if he lived for another hundred years.

As if in a daze, Annaliese seemed to have forgotten all about her desire to see the horses again until Max the stable keeper slid open the door and waved.

Annaliese came back to the moment. "Please, Miss Pine," she begged, "I want to visit the horses before we leave."

Miss Pine scanned the dark swollen clouds. "No, we have to get back."

Three or four new inches of snow already covered the ground.

Annaliese's bottom lip quivered. "But Great-Grandmama said that I could."

Miss Pine put her hands on her hips. "No. Not now. Not today."

Max was suddenly beside Annaliese.

"The horses . . . ," she said to him, pointing toward the stable.

Max stole a glance at the sky. "No, Miss Pine is right. You'd better be getting along now. This storm is going to be a real humdinger."

"I don't care," Annaliese said weakly.

"After the storm passes, I'll be taking the sleighs out for test runs. You let me know, little missy, if you'd like to ride along."

"How about tomorrow?" Annaliese put her mouth close to Throckmorton's ear. "Then we can visit Great-Grandmama again."

"I'll phone you up," Max promised, "as soon as the weather allows."

As they made their way back to the manor

house, frosty winds whipped across the meadow. Snowflakes whirled up, down, and around in a wild dance. A pine marten scurried across the quickly disappearing path.

Annaliese slipped and skidded in her mother's boots. She tried stepping in the indentations made by Miss Pine's footsteps, but she couldn't keep up. Crossing the footbridge, she took a tumble.

Miss Pine tried to help her up, but then she lost her footing too. She landed on Throckmorton and all but knocked the stuffing right out of him.

"Those boots!" Miss Pine snapped, brushing the snow off her coat. "I should have never allowed you to wear them."

Annaliese retrieved Throckmorton and gave him a good hard shake.

They forged ahead with the wind in their faces. Annaliese's eyebrows and eyelashes crusted with ice crystals. In the distance Throckmorton heard the *clinkety-clink, clinkety-clink* of tire chains turning and churning in new snow.

"Look!" Annaliese pointed as Eastcliff came into view.

A caravan of snow-covered automobiles, like igloos with amber eyes, was crawling up the lane. Tethered to his dog house, Donald the Great Dane barked and strained against his chain.

In the circular drive in front of Eastcliff, Teddy and Evan stopped shoveling when they saw Annaliese and Miss Pine coming. Teddy waved and cried out, "The aunties are coming! The aunties are coming!"

"And the storm of the century!" Evan yelled.

Evan lobbed a snowball that landed close to Miss Pine's feet. Miss Pine laughed and lobbed one back. Then Teddy got in the game. Soon balls of packed snow whizzed back and forth above Throckmorton's head.

A snowball, hurled with blazing speed, came straight at Miss Pine. She ducked. Annaliese, who was behind her, must not have seen it coming.

The snowball smacked Annaliese's face. The icy ball exploded.

She screamed. Her lip split open. A spray of scarlet red blood spurted from her nose.

Miss Pine lunged to Annaliese's side. She pressed her handkerchief onto her nose. "Tip your head back. It's a nosebleed. A split lip, too. Don't worry—you're going to be fine."

Throckmorton felt himself slip from Annaliese's grip, his body momentarily suspended in midair.

Oh-no-Oh-no-Oh-nooooo . . .

He glided through a swirl of giant snowflakes and landed in a snowy mound dotted with blood.

Throckmorton could hear a cacophony of car doors slamming and voices shouting, "What happened? What happened? Is she all right?"

And then . . .

A long cold stretch of silence.

A Cold Coffin

At first, Throckmorton lay calmly, fascinated by the unique architecture of each snowflake in the moment before it melted on his eye.

They were like him, he thought—one of a kind.

He assured himself that once the excitement died down, Evan or Teddy or maybe Annaliese herself would come looking for him.

Soon snowflakes—too many to count—masked his face.

Holy frozen rats!

They'd forgotten all about him . . .

Now every single snowflake felt like a stone.

Blanketed with heavy snow, Throckmorton sensed the passage of time; first dusk, then darkness. Sometime later, he heard Annaliese screech, "But I have to find Throckmorton! I can't leave him out there!"

Someone, maybe one of the aunties, shouted, "Get back in the house this minute! You'll never find him in all that snow!"

"I don't care. I'm going!"

"No! You'll freeze! It's too dangerous! Wait until morning!"

"Teddy and I'll go!" Evan shouted. "We'll tie ourselves together with a rope."

"Get Bailey!" Annaliese cried. "He'll find him!"

But after that Throckmorton heard no voices at all.

Throughout the night, the savage blizzard raged. Visions of Miss Beatrice and Sir Rudyard, lifeless in the black coffinlike instrument cases, haunted him.

I won't end up like them . . . I can't end up like them, he told himself over and over again.

He must stay awake and keep his sock monkey senses alive: eyes, ears, nose, and skin.

It was his only hope.

First, he counted forward.

Then, he counted backward.

Next, he created lists:

The names of the judge's seven sisters (Pansy, Patricia, Penelope, Petra, Pixie, Polly, Priscilla).

The kinds of pies that Mrs. Wiggins baked (lemon merengue, mince, rhubarb, cherry, pecan, pumpkin, banana cream).

The colors of the days-of-the-week ribbons Annaliese once wore in her hair, starting with Monday (lilac, butter yellow, persimmon, lime green, melon orange, petal pink, and periwinkle on Sundays).

Later, while reciting his cousins' names on Great-Grandmama's sock monkey family tree, he was stabbed by a new reality: If he wasn't found, he'd miss Great-Grandmama's birthday party!

He imagined the note of regret that he would write if he were able to use a pen:

~RSVP~

Mr. Throckmorton S. Monkey is buried in a snow bank. He deeply regrets that he will be unable to attend Ethel Constance Easterling's ninetieth birthday party.

Oh, the disappointment was cruel and impossible to bear.

Throckmorton fought the good fight for two more days and two more nights. Eventually, his body grew cold, his mind grew weary, and his spirit grew weak. He lost all track of time.

In his diminished state, he visualized the coming of spring. How the sky would spit showers of chilly rain. How Annaliese would find her beloved sock monkey soaked and misshapen in a slushy, muddy mess.

At long last, his heavy, unhappy thoughts sucked all the hope out of him. The battle was lost. He slept.

In his dreams, Throckmorton drifted off to a shimmering palace where red-heeled sock monkeys in tuxedos danced until dawn and (a very much alive) Miss Beatrice told him that his kisses tasted like red licorice.

Little by little, the moon-jeweled sky lightened to morning gray and the stars slipped out of sight. Throckmorton became aware—he didn't know how—of movement taking place above him.

A soft scraping sound thrummed in his dull ears. Snow crystals broke up before his black button eyes.

Smoo-sh! Squoo-sh!

A gigantic paw plunged into his snowy grave.

Then a second paw, with thick pads and curved nails, lunged past the first. The beast's feet clawed and scrabbled. Miraculously, Throckmorton's body parts were spared.

Finally, a huge square snout broke through.

Donald the Great Dane!

The gentle beast had broken off his chain.

The dog's breath smelled rank. His tongue was slimy. As his jaws snapped shut, Donald's incisors penetrated Throckmorton's stuffed head.

Yee-ouch!

Donald shimmied backwards out of the snow tunnel. In the silver-gray light, Eastcliff appeared as a ghost ship anchored in tall frozen waves.

The dog struggled through the deep, deep snow on long legs as unsteady as stilts. When they reached his dog house, he pawed aside a scrap of horse blanket that hung across the opening.

Donald's sleeping space smelled like straw. He cradled Throckmorton between his bony legs and laid his snout on Throckmorton's smile.

Donald's body heat warmed him. The *thump-thump-thump* of the dog's hammering heart made him feel safe. Dog slobber washed over him like a warm cleansing rain. He slept again.

Soon the hopeful sun rose higher in the morning sky. Donald clamped down on Throckmorton's leg with a soft mouth and shook him awake. Slowly, they scaled and conquered windswept drifts of snow, some as tall as Great-Grandmama's horses.

Throckmorton had spent most of his life feeling bendy and floppy or droopy and saggy. But at this moment, his heart swelled with gratitude so strong that it seemed as if he were truly made of muscles and bones.

Throckmorton had judged the canine species most unfairly and vowed never to do so again.

Outside the kitchen door, Donald let loose a crescendo of jubilant barks.

"Well, well, well . . . would you look at that?" Mrs. Wiggins marveled as she opened the door.

"Throckmorton! Praise be . . . you're just what the doctor ordered."

Snowed In

Pride burned in Donald's molasses-brown eyes. The Great Dane opened his powerful jaws and dropped Throckmorton at Mrs. Wiggins's feet. It was a soft landing.

Sprinkles of white flour dusted the cook's sturdy shoes. Her kingdom—Eastcliff's kitchen—smelled warm and rich and yeasty.

Her kitchen smelled like home.

A broad smile creased Mrs. Wiggins's face. She petted Donald's head and scratched his ears.

"No more outdoor dog house for you, good boy."

She dug a meaty shank bone out of the icebox and offered it to the grinning dog. She folded an old patchwork quilt and fashioned it into a dog bed in the corner by the stove.

"Well," she said with a shrug, "at least until Judge Easterling gets back from London."

Until the judge gets back from London?

Hip, hip, hooray!

Throckmorton hadn't missed the party after all.

The cook scooped Throckmorton up off the floor. She held him over the kitchen sink and shook off the clingy crystals of snow. "You're one naughty sock monkey, disappearing like that," she scolded.

She laid his body lengthwise across the pipes of a radiator. "Now, dry yourself out before I take you up to see Annaliese. Poor thing, she's been worried sick, as if she weren't sick enough already."

Annaliese was *sick*?

How sick?

The disturbing news took all the joy out of Throckmorton's resurrection.

The radiator's steam heat slowly saturated Throckmorton's stuffing. He heard Mrs. Wiggins humming as she kneaded dough for a loaf of bread, Donald chomping on the crunchy shank bone, and the crackle of a radio announcer's voice warning of postblizzard temperatures of twenty degrees below zero.

Then the telephone rang.

"Thank goodness," Mrs. Wiggins exclaimed, dashing to answer it.

Underneath Throckmorton, the radiator pipes were getting warmer.

Then hot.

Then hotter.

Soon puffs of steam rose up and around his damp body.

Take me off! he pleaded silently. My skin is singeing!

"Whoops!" Mrs. Wiggins hung up the phone.

She whisked Throckmorton off the radiator in the nick of time. She tucked his dry body under her arm, poured a cup of coffee, and placed it on the table in the breakfast nook.

Then she positioned Throckmorton upright on the bench across from where she sat.

"This is the situation," Mrs. Wiggins confided, as if they were the oldest and dearest of friends. "We're snowed in. We can't get out and the doctor can't get in. And Annaliese is as sick as any child I've ever seen." Her voice wavered. "Between you and me, Monkey, I'm worried."

Now Throckmorton was worried too.

Really worried.

"Not to mention, this birthday party . . . it's going to be the death of me. Those P sisters are the bossiest bunch of busybodies, why, I tell you."

Mrs. Wiggins rubbed her palms up and down her deeply wrinkled cheeks. "Yesterday, I blew my stack. Prudence, who's in charge of decorations and who I never did like, had the nerve—the nerve!— to imply that I had stolen the monogrammed silver candlesticks that went missing last Christmas."

Apparently Judge Easterling's sisters were carrying out Great-Grandmama's specific orders: Her ninetieth-birthday party must rival the splendor of those she'd once thrown at Eastcliff. When it came to honoring her sock monkeys, the P sisters were told to spare no expense.

"It's a cardinal sin," Mrs. Wiggins griped, "during times like these when folks are out of work and children are out begging."

Mrs. Wiggins carried Throckmorton up the once-elegant and greatly admired center hall staircase, pointing out all the recent changes.

Everywhere he looked, party preparations were under way.

In the foyer, the black-and-white marble tiles gleamed. Above the landing, the chandelier's crystals sparkled like thousands of tiny strikes of lightning. In their newly dusted picture frames, even Annaliese's grim ancestors seemed more cheerful.

On Eastcliff's second floor, the doors to the east and west wings—locked for years to save on heat—opened wide. Fires burned in the fireplaces of each and every bedroom they passed. For the first time since Olivia left, the manor house felt alive and downright toasty.

However, serious trouble roosted elsewhere.

Mrs. Wiggins tiptoed into Annaliese's bedroom.

Annaliese was in bed, propped against a stack of pillows. Her eyes were shut, her mouth open, and her head drooped to the side. Her split upper lip was still puffy. Scraggly strands of unwashed hair hung across the shoulders of her flannel nightgown.

Throckmorton's first thought was that his sweet keeper was—

No!

STOP!

Throckmorton wouldn't allow himself to even *think* the word.

Miss Pine sat in a rocking chair pulled close to Annaliese's bedside. Her heavy-lidded eyes lit up when she saw Throckmorton.

"Donald found him," Mrs. Wiggins said quietly. "Don't ask me where or how."

"That's the best news we've had in days."

"How is she?"

"Worse," Miss Pine replied. "A little while ago, the poor child tried to tell me something, but she started coughing so hard, she almost choked to death."

"The doctor phoned up," Mrs. Wiggins told the distraught nanny. "The county road will be plowed soon. I told Max to hitch up the horses, drive the sleigh down to the end of the lane, and wait for him."

Miss Pine dropped her voice to a whisper. "Shouldn't we try to reach Judge Easterling? What if . . ."

"A fat lot of good his worrying's going to do. Worry doesn't count for much when a child's as sick as this one."

Miss Pine drew Throckmorton's body out of the cook's hands and pulled back the bedcovers. "Perhaps if she knows that her sock monkey's been found . . ."

Imagine his shock when Throckmorton spied Sir Rudyard lying on Annaliese's left side and Miss Beatrice on her right. Captain Eugene slept peacefully on her stomach.

Throckmorton couldn't contain his jealousy.

What were *they* doing in *his* spot with *his* keeper?

Miss Pine nudged Annaliese, but couldn't rouse her.

Wake up! Wake up! Throckmorton pleaded with every thread of his being. It's me . . . I'm home . . .

Miss Pine lifted Captain Eugene off Annaliese's stomach and shifted him and Sir Rudyard into spots next to Miss Beatrice. Then she nestled Throckmorton into the crook of Annaliese's left arm, right next to her heart.

Annaliese's breathing sounded labored. A moist pungent heat radiated through damp diaper cloths packed on her chest. Her cough made a harsh, brittle, heartbreaking sound.

Not good, Throckmorton despaired. Not good at all.

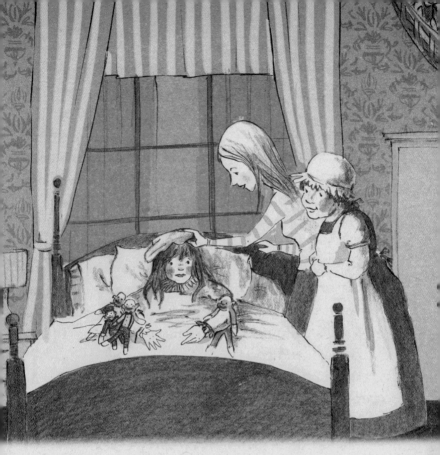

Finally, Annaliese opened her eyes and smiled feebly.

"Donald found your sock monkey," Miss Pine said tenderly. "You don't have to worry anymore. Throckmorton's here to help you get well."

Dr. Webb came and went. Double pneumonia, he determined. With the arctic temperatures and icy roads, he didn't want to risk taking Annaliese to the hospital forty miles away.

He left a bottle of medicine, but warned Miss Pine: "It's no magic potion." There were different kinds of pneumonia, he explained: the kind that medicine would help and the kind that it wouldn't.

"She's sailing in dangerous waters," he added. "It's touch and go."

Mrs. Wiggins suggested strongly that Great-Grandmama's birthday party—a little more than a week away—be canceled.

Cancel the sock monkeys' party?

The pain of Throckmorton's disappointment was so searing that he almost passed out.

Fortunately, Dr. Webb disagreed. "If Annaliese pulls through, having something to look forward to will help her heal."

What did the doctor mean—*if* she pulls through?

Later, while Annaliese slept and Miss Pine dozed in the rocking chair, Captain Eugene told Throckmorton about everything he'd missed during the three nights and two days he'd been buried in the snowbank.

"I was in Teddy's bedroom and could hear Annaliese calling for you. Teddy figured that Annaliese was too sick to tell one sock monkey from the other, so Teddy undressed me and then tucked me into her bed.

"Annaliese wasn't fooled. She kept yelling, 'Throckmorton! Throckmorton!'

"So, Evan took off Sir Rudyard's clothes and nestled his body next to mine. Annaliese clung to us, but still kept calling for you. Then Miss Pine brought her Miss Beatrice.

"We've been by her side day and night," Captain Eugene proudly concluded.

Grateful to his comrades, Throckmorton shed his earlier envy.

Sock monkeys to the rescue . . . *Huzzah!*

"I've been hugged so much, I feel like a new monkey."

Throckmorton's ears perked.

That wasn't Captain Eugene's voice . . . that was Sir Rudyard speaking!

Sir Rudyard—emerged from his senseless state, and bragging to boot!

Miss Beatrice, Throckmorton noticed, also emitted sparks of sock monkey soul. Traces of luster glimmered in her jingle-bell eyes. Her smile curled up slightly at the corners.

And then he heard Miss Beatrice's voice for the first time outside of his dreams. "Hello, Throckmorton," she said shyly. "We're happy to have you home."

What a surprising turn of events. Throckmorton wouldn't have believed it if he hadn't heard it with his own ears and seen it with his own eyes.

As sick as she was, Annaliese's loving touch had brought the abandoned sock monkeys back to their senses.

Moments later, Miss Pine woke up. "What time is it?"

She leaned over and pressed her palm to Annaliese's forehead. Her eyes filled with fear. "Oh no!"

Miss Pine shook Annaliese's shoulders. "Annaliese, wake up. I need to take your temperature. Slip the thermometer under your tongue. Yes, that's right."

The time waiting for the thermometer to stop rising felt like an eternity.

"104.4!" Miss Pine cried as Mrs. Wiggins rushed into the room. "Call Dr. Webb! Tell him to come back NOW."

Miss Pine pressed cold compresses on Annaliese's neck, cheeks, and brow. Her breathing sounded even more raspy and shallow than it had just hours before. Every time she coughed, she winced with pain.

"We can't wait for the doctor," Miss Pine told Mrs. Wiggins. "We've got to bring the fever down somehow . . . the medicine's not working."

"Run a tepid bath," Mrs. Wiggins said, "and make it quick."

Miss Pine looked doubtful, but Mrs. Wiggins wouldn't be dissuaded. "A cool bath's what saved my wee sister's life."

As the nanny undressed her charge, Throckmorton's heart sickened. Without her nightgown, Annaliese's body seemed so slight, as though a part of her was already on its way to another world.

Throckmorton felt like a wretched failure. He'd let Annaliese down.

Foolishly he'd believed that his love, loyalty, listening, and never-ending smile would always help, always heal, and always give hope.

If there'd ever been a time for Throckmorton to do something remarkable, the time was now.

Instead, a serpentine voice slithered into his mind: *You're only a sock monkey. You can't do anything.*

With a sunken spirit, he watched Miss Pine carry Annaliese off to the bathroom. Mrs. Wiggins set the four sock monkeys on the rocking chair and stripped the bed of its rumpled sheets.

Throckmorton heard a soft knocking. Evan poked his head around the bedroom door and Mrs. Wiggins waved him in.

Evan spied Annaliese's empty bed. His face drained of color. He stood motionless, his fists clenched.

Evan's eyes shifted from one corner of the room to the other. "Where is she? What's wrong?"

Mrs. Wiggins took hold of Evan's arm to steady him. "Don't worry. Your sister's in the bath. Miss Pine is with her. Everything's going to be all right."

Evan opened his right hand. "I have something to give her."

Throckmorton's eyes caught a glimpse of gold.

Could it be . . . ?

Yes, it was!

Olivia's locket!

"Wh—where," Mrs. Wiggins stammered, "did you find that?"

"Will you give it to her?" Evan asked. "I think she'd like to have it."

"I will." Mrs. Wiggins nodded. "I promise."

Evan seemed reluctant to leave.

"Get on back to bed now, Evan," Mrs. Wiggins urged. "Your sister's in the Good Lord's hands now. There's nothing we mortals can do . . ." She slipped the locket into her apron pocket and pulled out her rosary. "Except pray."

Mrs. Wiggins lined Throckmorton, Captain Eugene, Sir Rudyard, and Miss Beatrice against a shammed pillow. She held her palm against the middle of her back, eased herself into the rocking chair, and let her hands drop down limp between her knees.

The clock's pendulum swung back and forth, a maddening and persistent *tick-tock*, *tick-tock*, *tick-tock*.

Why didn't Miss Pine bring Annaliese back to bed? Throckmorton fretted. What was taking so long? Where was the doctor?

Mrs. Wiggins fingered the necklace's gleaming chain. Then she clicked the locket's tiny clasp and drew the miniature photos close to her face. Soon Throckmorton could see that the old woman's eyelashes were wet.

Mrs. Wiggins dabbed her eyes with her hanky. She wrapped Olivia's locket in the tear-stained square of cloth and tucked it into the well of the lamp on Annaliese's nightstand.

She made the sign of the cross on her chest.

"For safekeeping," she told the sock monkeys, "until Annaliese gets better."

During that long, seemingly endless night and

into the next day, Annaliese lingered between life and death.

Throckmorton, Captain Eugene, Sir Rudyard, and Miss Beatrice took turns keeping watch.

No matter how helpless and inadequate they felt on the inside, their smiles never wavered.

And finally, Annaliese's fever broke.

Birth of the Blues

For the next three days as Annaliese recuperated, Miss Pine and Mrs. Wiggins often left her alone to sleep. A large dose of rest and time, Dr. Webb advised, was the best medicine.

Throckmorton, Captain Eugene, Sir Rudyard, and Miss Beatrice enjoyed a long-overdue family reunion at her bedside. The sock monkeys relished this rare opportunity to share secrets, tell stories, and yes, repeat juicy gossip about their keepers.

Captain Eugene had the biggest stash of information, but Throckmorton held a luscious secret: Ebenezer the Lighthouse Keeper, whom they'd meet at Great-Grandmama's party, had a giant diamond buried inside his heart. *(Maybe they all did!)*

Throckmorton decided that he'd let the others chatter, chatter, chatter . . . until the moment was right. Then, when the spotlight was his and his alone, he'd tell all.

One night, Sir Rudyard asked Captain Eugene if he knew what had really happened between Olivia and the judge.

Captain Eugene was ever-so-happy to tell them.

"Annaliese was only a few months old," he explained, "when the housekeeper moved Evan and Teddy into that baby-blue bedroom across the hall from the nursery. Teddy and I slept in one bed. Evan slept alone in the other. I remember Evan telling Teddy at the time that Sir Rudyard was lost. One night, Olivia came in to say good night. But instead of a bringing a storybook, she was carrying a suitcase."

"What kind of suitcase?" Throckmorton asked.

Captain Eugene hated to be interrupted. He ignored the question and carried on with his tale. "'Mommy has to go away for a little while,' Olivia

told the boys. 'Be good, and take care of your baby sister until I get back.'

"Olivia must have planned to leave in secret, but suddenly, the judge charged into the twins' bedroom. He wrenched the suitcase out of her hand. 'You came with nothing, you leave with nothing,' he told her."

"But it still doesn't explain *why* Olivia left," said Throckmorton.

"You know how it is with us monkeys," Captain Eugene lamented. "We observe. We eavesdrop. Then our keepers move out of range. We may hear the beginning, middle, or end, but rarely do we hear a whole story. It's really quite frustrating."

"Sock monkeys should get to live their own stories," Sir Rudyard asserted. "What good is seeing and hearing and smelling if we can't *do* anything?"

"If I had a choice," said Miss Beatrice, "I'd rather *be* someone than do something."

Sir Rudyard scoffed. "So, tell me, Miss Be . . . how did you like *be-ing* in the mandolin case? How's it been for you, *be-ing* the judge's sock monkey?"

"It couldn't have been easy . . . ," Throckmorton empathized.

"It wasn't," Miss Beatrice agreed. "The judge was a nasty rat of a child, much like Evan can be, I daresay."

"In what way?" asked Throckmorton.

"Born with a silver spoon in his mouth," she said, "but no mother to feed him."

"You mean the judge's mother ran off too?" Captain Eugene asked.

"So to speak," answered Miss Beatrice. "The judge's mother, Margaret, didn't care for a dull life on an isolated estate like Eastcliff-by-the-Sea. She preferred London. For the most part, he and his seven sisters were raised by the household help."

Hmmm . . . never once had Throckmorton considered the possibility that Judge Easterling had had his own set of heartaches as a child.

"So, tell me, how did you end up in the mandolin case?" Captain Eugene asked Miss Beatrice.

"Olivia put me there, along with that locket."

"She put me in the violin case," said Sir Rudyard.

"But why?" questioned Throckmorton. "None of this makes any sense."

"Perhaps Olivia was trying to keep us safe," Sir Rudyard suggested.

"I agree," said Captain Eugene. "Olivia must have known what happened to Easterling sock monkeys—like you and Miss Beatrice—who aren't cherished by their keepers."

Miss Beatrice stared off into the distance.

"What are you thinking?" Throckmorton kindly inquired of her.

"Olivia was like the moon," Miss Beatrice replied. "She had two sides: one dark, one light. She was odd, but enchanting. Young and yet old beyond her years." She paused to collect her thoughts. "I believe the judge was drawn to Olivia's light, but confused by her darkness."

"Olivia spent hours hand-stitching the little wedding gown for me," Miss Beatrice continued. "Right before she closed the mandolin case, she whispered, 'It's over.'"

"A ritual of sorts," Sir Rudyard opined.

How strange, Throckmorton thought.

"After Annaliese was born," Captain Eugene recalled, "Olivia seemed very sad—and very much alone. She sighed and cried and said sorrowful things like 'Such a secret place . . . this land of tears.'"

Sir Rudyard confirmed that Olivia had changed dramatically—especially after the judge barred her friends from coming to Eastcliff to play music. "He called her bandmates 'riffraff'—country bumpkins whose music was nothing but noise; it gave him a headache."

"I guess no one really knows the truth," Captain Eugene concluded. "Some people said that Olivia ran off with another man; others swore that her brother came to Eastcliff and took her back to the place where they grew up."

"Where's that?" asked Throckmorton.

"The Black Forest," Captain Eugene answered. "In a country called Germany."

"Funny how two such different people could end up together," Throckmorton mused.

"You know what they say. . . ." Miss Beatrice smiled her charming, off-center smile. "Opposites attract."

The talkative sock monkeys now heard the sound of footsteps and instantly fell silent.

Annaliese stirred.

Miss Pine walked into Annaliese's room carrying a cup of hot tea with slices of lemon ringing the saucer.

Annaliese rubbed the sleep out of her eyes. "I had the strangest dream, Miss Pine. The sock monkeys were talking about my mother. Isn't that odd? I wish I could remember what they said. . . ."

"They do indeed seem real sometimes," Miss Pine acknowledged.

"They're like spies—the good kind," Annaliese agreed. "I bet they know all of our secrets."

The first week of February passed into the second. Throckmorton, Captain Eugene, Sir Rudyard, and Miss Beatrice had less time to socialize as Annaliese spent more time awake.

It was Sunday, they heard Miss Pine say. The aunties had gone back to their own homes, leaving long lists of things for her, Mrs. Wiggins, and the recently hired help to do. The judge's seven sisters planned to return in a few days, on Thursday, with their families in tow, to oversee the final party preparations.

Once again, Annaliese asked Miss Pine if she could go visit Great-Grandmama. Once again, Miss Pine said no.

"You're not strong enough. And your great-grandmother is under the weather as well."

Miss Pine had good reason to be concerned.

Annaliese's pale skin resembled frosted glass. She'd coughed so hard and so often that she'd injured her ribs. She dressed each morning, but was still too weak to take her meals downstairs. Mrs. Wiggins brought up a tray, but most of the food remained on her plate, skillfully rearranged.

Worry nibbled away at Throckmorton's soft stuffing.

Great-Grandmama's birthday party was less than a week away. What if his keeper wasn't well enough to attend?

And then, unbeknownst to anyone else, Madge hinted to Annaliese that the severity of Great-Grandmama's medical condition was being swept under the carpet.

"How bad is she?" Annaliese asked in a terror-stricken tone of voice.

"Who knows?" said Madge slyly. "But we hope she pulls through; otherwise Her Highness's birthday party ball might turn into an awfully fancy funeral."

Oh, how Throckmorton hated that lazy maid. . . .

On Monday afternoon, Evan and Teddy burst into Annaliese's bedroom. "A ten-piece orchestra called the Bird Land Big Band will be playing at the party," Teddy announced. "Great-Grandmama hired them and it's costing a fortune."

"But here's the big news," said Evan. "We just found out! The aunties made up a new rule—but they forgot to tell us."

"A new rule?" Annaliese asked.

"We have to come to Great-Grandmama's party in costumes." Evan wrinkled his nose. "How dumb is that?"

"But why?"

Evan imitated his Aunt Petra's hands-on-hips stance and snippy tone of voice. "Our sock monkeys have costumes, why shouldn't we? Why should *they* have all the fun?"

Not all the sock monkeys have costumes, Throckmorton wanted to say. He didn't, and neither did Miss Beatrice.

"That's not the only reason," said Teddy. "Aunt Priscilla told me that our relatives from the Midwest are dreadfully dull. Costumes will liven things up."

Evan grinned at Teddy. "Maybe Uncle Fred will spike the punch."

"Liven things up?" Annaliese sputtered. "Madge told me that Great-Grandmama was dying."

"Nonsense!" Teddy laughed. "She's got a bad cold, that's all."

Annaliese's face brightened. "Really? A bad cold—that's all?"

Teddy nodded.

"Still," she said after a few moments, "it's Great-Grandmama's birthday party—not a costume party. It's Valentine's Day—not Halloween."

Teddy agreed. "Mrs. Wiggins warned them: 'Great-Grandmama isn't going to like this.' Aunt Petra wouldn't budge. 'Nonsense. . . . We'll surprise her. She'll love it!'"

"Not a chance," said Evan. "Great-Grandmama expects everyone to play by her rules—they ought to know that by now."

Throckmorton was appalled. Suddenly it seemed as if their keepers were more important than the sock monkeys themselves.

Hadn't the party invitation been addressed to him, not Annaliese? To Miss Beatrice, not the judge?

On the other hand, he figured that if everyone was coming in costume, then Annaliese would also have to find him something special to wear, wouldn't she?

He imagined how splendid he'd look dressed as a distinguished knight in shining armor or a French painter with a palette, brush, and black beret.

"What are you going to wear?" Annaliese asked Teddy.

"I'm going to be a pirate who's looted Captain Eugene's ship."

"How about you, Evan?"

"It's a surprise," he answered with an evasive smile.

Just then Miss Pine glided into the room, eyes shining and cheeks flushed. "Annaliese," she said, "I've decided to make Miss Beatrice an outfit for Great-Grandmama's party."

"What kind?"

"A Scottish girl, right and proper." Miss Pine drew Miss Beatrice into her arms. "Plaid, I think. With a tam. And, if you don't mind, I'd like to borrow that sewing basket."

Great-Grandmama's chintz-lined wicker basket, along with a get-well card, had been delivered to Annaliese a few days earlier.

"Sure, okay, I guess."

As Miss Pine whisked out of Annaliese's bedroom, a piece of folded paper fluttered to the floor.

Evan snatched it up. "What's this?"

Annaliese snapped to attention. "It's mine! Give it to me."

Evan unfolded the note.

"I would like you to have this," he read aloud. "Perhaps someday you'll decide to keep my sock monkey legacy alive. Please get well and don't worry. Guard our secret and someday your story will have a happy ending."

"What story?" Evan demanded.

"None of your business."

"You've always been lousy at keeping secrets, Annaliese," he reminded her. "I'll get it out of you one way or another."

"No you won't. Not this one," Annaliese retorted.

"Knock it off, Evan." Teddy snatched the note and flipped it to his sister. He scooped up Captain Eugene and then pressed Sir Rudyard into Evan's chest. "Come on, let's go. I'll race you to the kitchen. Winner gets the leftover piece of cherry pie!"

On Wednesday, Miss Pine returned the sewing basket to Annaliese. She brought all three sock monkeys along.

"Your father just phoned," she told Annaliese. "He's in Portland. He and your grandmother will be back from London late tomorrow night."

Miss Pine had freshened up Miss Beatrice's sock covering, repaired her eyelashes, and restitched her smile. Miss Beatrice's new clothes, she explained, were the colors of the Easterling coat of arms.

Captain Eugene's peacoat was brushed and the tiny brass buttons polished to a glossy luster. Sir Rudyard's bow tie was crisply knotted and his white shirt, paisley vest, and herringbone slacks freshly pressed.

Throckmorton was on fire. . . .

Didn't Annaliese understand how desperately *he* wanted to dress stylishly for Great-Grandmama's grand birthday party ball?

Why, it was high time to stop thinking only about herself and consider his feelings in the matter!

But what could he do?

He was only a sock monkey. . . .

A completely unremarkable sock monkey with a yellow duck diaper pin stuck to his chest.

Asleep and lost in a dense fog of disturbing dreams, Throckmorton searched for the perfect costume. He wandered into vast closets trying on kings' crowns and jesters' caps. A fairy with gauzy green wings draped a white ermine cape across his shoulders. A hunchbacked hangman slipped a noose around his neck.

Then, the scratch of a match.

Throckmorton sensed the presence of someone lurking in Annaliese's room.

He snapped awake.

In the dim candlelight, two figures hovered over Annaliese's bed: Judge Easterling, his overcoat unbuttoned; and Miss Pine, her chenille bathrobe drawn tightly shut.

Annaliese's breathing made a steady *whoosh, whoosh, whoosh* in and out, out and in. Throckmorton lay in her arms, which felt as thin as twigs.

The judge looked haggard; he hadn't shaved. He spoke in a hoarse whisper. "Explain, Miss Pine. I don't understand what's gone on here."

"The fever has passed. Her lungs are clear.

She suffers from a slight cough, but that's to be expected."

"Good grief."

"We did our best, sir."

The judge looked rattled.

"What next?" He heaved a deep sigh. "My house has been taken over by relatives whom I don't like. It's decorated like a Barnum and Bailey circus. And now this: my own daughter whom I barely recognize."

Miss Pine stood as strong as the sturdy trunk of a tall tree. "Give it time, sir," she urged, keeping her voice low. "Now that you're home, you'll see. Annaliese will soon be her old self again. And before you know it, the party will be over."

"Well, if those loopy sisters of mine think that I'm wearing a costume to my grandmother's ninetieth birthday party on Valentine's Day . . . they're badly mistaken."

"I'm sorry. I didn't mean to upset you," Miss Pine apologized. "I shouldn't have said anything. It wasn't my place."

Briefly she stepped out of the room and returned with her hands hidden behind her back. "Speaking of costumes . . ."

"I'd rather not."

"Here," she said softly, placing Miss Beatrice into the judge's arms.

"What's this?"

"Your sock monkey."

The pattern of Annaliese's breathing changed. Throckmorton could tell that she'd wakened, but she didn't open her eyes.

Miss Pine's fingers grazed Miss Beatrice's tartan shawl. "I made a new outfit for her, for the party."

The judge fell silent.

Bits and pieces of Throckmorton's stuffing turned to knots. Had Miss Pine overstepped her bounds?

The judge held Miss Beatrice close to the lit candle. The golden flame illuminated his sock monkey's transformation. Miss Beatrice's jingle bell eyes tinkled sweetly.

Cracks appeared in the judge's frozen face. "Thank you," he said quietly. "Thank you . . . for everything."

The radiator clanked, promising steam heat to scare away the chill of a winter's night.

Judge Easterling and Miss Pine stood at Annaliese's bedside—each waiting, or so it seemed, for the other to say good night.

Miss Beatrice filled the space between them.

Annaliese's fingers twitched. She raised one of her eyelids ever-so-slightly.

The judge made his next move awkwardly. He took one step forward . . . held out his left arm . . .

And then . . .

Egad!

He hugged Miss Pine!

Not very tightly . . . but even so . . .

Annaliese's body tensed. She stifled the sound that almost escaped from her mouth.

Trapped within their clumsy embrace, Miss Beatrice beamed.

Miss Beatrice S. Monkey: Sock Monkey Matchmaker!

Throckmorton waited for the inevitable. Annaliese's nanny would blush, turn, and walk away.

But Miss Pine didn't flinch.

"I'm sorry," the judge murmured, pulling back. His face was as scarlet as a sock monkey's smile.

"No need," said Miss Pine.

"It's just that . . ."

She nodded. "I understand."

"After such a long trip . . . coming home to chaos . . . seeing Annaliese sick like this . . . I'm not, I'm not thinking straight."

Miss Pine patted the pom-pom on Miss Beatrice's tam. "Let's agree to agree that the sock monkey made you do it, shall we?"

The shamefaced judge smiled.

Miss Pine traced the outline of Miss Beatrice's newly repaired smile. "They're highly contagious."

"Indeed," he replied.

Throckmorton grimaced. What was Miss Pine thinking?

Just a few short weeks ago, Judge Easterling couldn't even recall her name!

Annaliese rolled over, rustling her bedcovers.

Quickly, Miss Pine straightened her spine, dusted the front of her robe, smoothed the collar, and tightened the sash. "I'm glad you like her, sir."

"Are you coming to Great-Grandmama's birthday party, Miss Pine?"

"Yes—I mean, no." She looked off to the side. "I'll be working, of course."

"Of course."

"And about Annaliese, sir . . . her cousins, Petra's daughters, arrived this afternoon. I've invited them to a tea party tomorrow in Annaliese's room," she explained. "I thought it would be a good idea for her to spend time with girls her own age."

A tea party? Throckmorton grumbled to himself.

Annaliese should be putting his costume together, not wasting precious time at tea parties.

Miss Pine lifted the candle snuffer and extinguished the flame.

"Annaliese doesn't want to wear a costume

either—I'm not sure why," she told the judge. "I'm hoping she'll change her mind."

A wisp of smoke rose into the charged air.

"Like father, like daughter, it seems."

"Perhaps you'll change your mind, too, sir."

"Absolutely not."

He headed toward the door with a shudder. "I've never liked pretending that I'm someone else."

"No, sir. Indeed not, sir," Miss Pine agreed.

Tea Party

Midday on Friday, Miss Pine set four places at the tiny lace-covered table in the corner of Annaliese's room. Throckmorton was pleased to see that she was using his favorite doll dishes, the ones with daffodils and aqua rabbits.

"I've invited their sock monkeys as well," said Miss Pine with a wink in his direction.

Oh, what a happy day it was turning out to be!

Throckmorton had never met Nora's, Nadine's, and Nell Ann's sock monkeys, but he was eager to do so.

Annaliese seemed genuinely excited to see her cousins as well. She slipped on a new freshly pressed party dress. She also reminded Throckmorton that in less than forty-eight hours she'd get to see Great-Grandmama Easterling again.

Bluish glimmers of hope flickered in Annaliese's gray-green eyes. "Before the night is over," she vowed, "I'll get her to tell me the whole story."

On a larger table, also set for four, a three-tier silver serving dish held dainty petit fours and finger sandwiches cut into hearts, diamonds, clubs, and spades. Devonshire cream, lemon curd, and rosy-red jam accompanied a basket of freshly baked currant scones.

"Come along now, Throckmorton. It's almost time for tea." Miss Pine positioned her fingers under his arms and seated him at the tiny table. "Nora, Nadine, and Nell Ann will be here any minute."

Giggling loudly, three brown-haired girls—triplets—entered the bedroom, empty-handed.

Oh crumbs!

He'd been stood up!

In not so many words, the sisters made it clear to Miss Pine that they were city girls who considered tea parties with stuffed toys a thing of the past.

Annaliese joined them at the big table. Her pink ruffled puffed-sleeve dress hung like a sack on her bony body.

The cousins, who wore knee socks, pleated skirts, and matching sweaters, rolled their eyes in well-practiced, perfect harmony.

Annaliese's cousins jabbered about dreamy boys, spiffy clothes, and swanky homes. They ignored Throckmorton. Annaliese didn't even pretend to fill his cup with pretend tea.

"Where are your sock monkeys?" Annaliese asked the girl with bobbed hair whose name was Nadine.

"I shouldn't really be telling you this . . . ," Nadine

said. "You can keep a secret, can't you?"

Oh no! Not another secret!

"Well, a couple of years ago," Nadine explained, "the Ladies' Missionary Society at our church sponsored a toy drive. Bless her heart; Mother gave our sock monkeys to poor starving children living in China."

China? Throckmorton reminded himself to ask Captain Eugene where China was, and if they had any hopes of seeing those sock monkey cousins again.

"I mean, it wasn't as if we played with them any longer," said Nell Ann, flipping the rolled ends of her pageboy haircut.

Annaliese sent a sympathetic glance in Throckmorton's direction. "Didn't that make you sad?" she asked.

"Not really," said Nadine. "Great-Grandmama's sock monkeys were smelly."

"Woolly and scratchy," said Nora.

"And so-o-o old-fashioned," said Nell Ann.

"Then who's taking you to Great-Grandmama's birthday party?" Annaliese asked. "Only the sock monkeys got invitations. . . . We're going as their guests."

After insisting that the information was top secret, Nell Ann described how after the invitation arrived, their mother, Annaliese's Aunt Petra, had frantically traveled up and down the East Coast trying to locate suitable replacements in second-hand stores.

Annaliese, suddenly ravenous, devoured two scones, four little sandwiches, and three petit fours while she listened to Nell Ann's story.

"And did she find replacements?" Annaliese asked.

The girls nodded.

"Are they wearing the outfits that Great-Grandmama made for the originals?"

"Not exactly," said Nora. "Mother says that Great-Grandmama is half-blind; she'll never notice the difference."

They were wrong, dead wrong, Throckmorton protested.

Didn't they know that their sock monkeys' names were inscribed on the family tree that now hung above Great-Grandmama's fireplace? And, that she'd recorded detailed descriptions of their one-of-a-kind outfits in her leather-bound ledger?

As soon as Great-Grandmama realizes that Aunt Petra's daughters are frauds and their sock monkeys are fakes, she'll cut them out of her will for sure.

And it would serve them right! Throckmorton thought spitefully.

"So, Annaliese," said Nell Ann, switching the subject. "What are you going to be? We're dying to see your costume."

"Or," Nadine tittered, "are you wearing what you have on?"

"I don't have . . . uh, I mean . . . ," Annaliese faltered. "I don't want to show anyone just yet."

"Why not?" asked Nora.

"It's a surprise," she told them. "What about you?"

"We're going as jungle cats, with matching cubs," said Nora. "Mother made me a leopard costume."

"Mother made me a tiger costume," said Nell Ann.

"And I'm going as a lioness," said Nadine, scratching the air with painted fingernails. "Me-oww."

Looking mighty pleased with her catty self, Nadine set her napkin to the side of her dessert plate. "Excuse us, Annaliese, but we really must be going."

As she passed, Nadine plucked Throckmorton out of his chair and pointed at his diaper pin.

Annaliese's cousins didn't need to say a word. Their cruel eyes told the whole story.

After they left, Annaliese bit her lips, trying to hold back the tears that wanted to escape.

What kind of costume would Olivia have made Annaliese, Throckmorton wondered, if she were still here?

Something beautiful, he imagined.

Something blue.

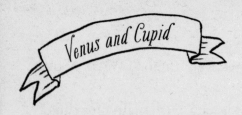

Venus and Cupid

"I'll show them," Annaliese vowed, shaking a pair of sewing scissors clenched in her fist. "If I can make a sock monkey, I can sew a costume, too."

Throckmorton couldn't have been more delighted . . .

If Annaliese made a costume for herself, then surely—surely—she'd make one for him, too, wouldn't she?

Yay, hooray!

Yellow duck diaper pin be gone!

Gritting her teeth, Annaliese quickly laid out her supplies. Her cheeks had a pinkish color—a good sign, Throckmorton decided.

Annaliese ran her fingers across the spines of books on her bookshelf. She selected the dark green one with the bold gold title, a collection of Greek myths that Miss Pine often read aloud.

Annaliese turned to a lavishly colored page.

"I shall be Venus and you shall be my Cupid," she told Throckmorton. She put her finger on a picture of a lovely woman with long hair and a flowing gown. "Venus is the goddess of love and Cupid is her son. Perfect for a Valentine's party!"

Cupid? Did she mean that naked baby with wings?

Holy doughnut holes!

How humiliating . . .

Annaliese seemed to sense his disappointment. "You'll get to carry a bow and a quiver full of arrows . . ."

She must have made another trip to the attic sometime, because now she displayed for him an assortment of items that she had found up there: a length of gold cord, Indian arrowheads, a stuffed seagull, and a hunting knife in a leather sheath.

Then Annaliese pulled the large dress box out from under her bed. From it she removed the damaged wedding gown.

Annaliese measured her arm with a marked tape. Next she measured the gown's lace sleeves. With a *snip-snip-snip* of the sewing shears, she cut the sleeves to size.

Annaliese peeked at the clock with the painted face that hung on the wall. "I don't have time to hem them," she lamented. "It's almost time for dinner."

Determining the correct length for the skirt proved to be more difficult. Ultimately, Annaliese threw aside the tape measure. Trying her best to follow a straight line, she cut a swath of fabric off the entire bottom of the skirt.

She disappeared to dine downstairs, and when she returned to her room, she put on the dress. The top, Throckmorton noticed, was too big. The skirt was too long. She clipped off a few more inches and tried it on again. In the end, the length looked just right in the front, but too short in the back.

"Oh well, the veil will cover that."

Annaliese spread a long tulle-and-lace veil across the floor.

Throckmorton could see that a small section of fabric had been cut out of the veil as well.

Working with unyielding determination, Annaliese trimmed the veil and fashioned it into a cape. Then she tucked and pinned and stitched until the rest of the dress fit.

Sort of.

Annaliese stepped in front of her full-length mirror and wrapped the gold cord around her waist. She looked like an angel, albeit one that had fallen from the sky.

The clock struck nine.

Bedtime! A look of panic crossed Annaliese's face. She was able to hide everything in her closet just before the judge stopped in to say good night.

The next morning, on Valentine's Day, Annaliese got up early to make Throckmorton's costume. Under the circumstances, working on Venus and

Cupid costumes in secret was not so easy.

Eastcliff-by-the-Sea was like a fortress under siege. Catering trucks filled with exotic foods lumbered up the lane. Bouquets of freshly cut flowers spilled out of florists' vans. Musical instruments in black cases tumbled out of the Bird Land Big Band's touring bus.

A discordant mixture of sounds echoed within Eastcliff's walls—a high-spirited mixture of pounding footsteps, breaking dishes, barking dogs, confusion, and short tempers.

Meanwhile, Annaliese created sock-monkey-sized arrows out of long pencils and thumb-sized Indian arrowheads. She used a wooden hanger without a hook for Cupid's bow. The leather knife sheath would serve as Cupid's quiver.

She stretched leftover swatches of bridal veil over curved pieces of wire. She plucked feathers from the tail and wings of the stuffed seagull and glued them onto Cupid's wings.

The clock chimed three times. Only three hours till the party!

Annaliese crossed her fingers. "I hope your wings dry in time."

Throckmorton hoped they didn't.

No sock monkey in his right mind would be caught dead in that hideous outfit.

Annaliese drew down the window shades as the afternoon sunshine faded. "It's time to get ready!"

Annaliese slipped on a pair of ballet slippers, fluffed her hair, and pinched her cheeks. Then she made a few minor adjustments to Cupid's costume.

He waited for her to remove his diaper pin, but she didn't.

Perhaps just as well . . .

Throckmorton would probably feel lost without it.

When Annaliese held Throckmorton up to the tall mirror, this is what he saw: a red-heeled sock monkey named Cupid who looked utterly, stupendously stupid.

Woe, oh, woe, was he . . .

But then at the peak of his embarrassment, a miracle occurred.

The goddess of love laughed.

All of a sudden Throckmorton didn't care how stupid he looked.

He'd bear his humiliation bravely, because, stupid or not, Cupid had pierced Annaliese's heart and made her smile.

Saturday, February 14th . . .

Six o'clock in the evening . . .

The Ballroom . . .

Eastcliff-by-the-Sea . . .

The moment that Mr. Throckmorton S. Monkey and forty-eight other hand-sewn, red-heeled sock monkeys had been waiting for had arrived!

Ethel Constance Easterling's ninetieth-birthday party!

Hallelujah!

Decked out in their fragile costumes, Annaliese and Throckmorton sat next to each other on the cushioned bench in front of her bedroom's bay window, waiting for the party guests to arrive.

The evening's first stars graced a lavender sky. A snow moon lingered above an outline of trees softened by dusk. Crystal-white snowflakes sifted down, like promises, frosting the sill.

Flames from giant torches illuminated the snow-covered lane. Huge red velvet hearts hung on bare branches for as far as the eye could see. Max Wiggins came into view, driving a team of the magnificent Clydesdales. White puffs of breath wreathed the horses' heads.

Annaliese opened the window a crack. The jingle of sleigh bells strapped to the horses' necks mingled with gay laughter rising out of a sleigh full of party guests.

Miss Pine, who wore a white blouse and straight black skirt, hustled into Annaliese's room, calling, "Time to join the party!" Mrs. Wiggins followed closely behind.

Holding Throckmorton in two hands like a bridal bouquet, Annaliese took tentative steps toward the door.

"I'm trying not to trip," she told them.

"Turn around." Miss Pine drew a circle in air. "Let me see your costume. You made that yourself? I can't believe it . . . it's wonderful!"

"And you!" Miss Pine pinched Throckmorton's soft cheek. "You look *amazing*!"

"Annaliese, before you go downstairs," the cook said kindly, "I have a surprise for you."

"You do? What is it?"

"It's a present—something that Evan wanted you to have."

Mrs. Wiggins leaned over Annaliese's nightstand and eased Olivia's locket out of the lamp's well. Her lips curled into a thin smile as she pressed the treasure into Annaliese's outstretched hand.

The locket's jewels sparkled, but not as brightly as Annaliese's eyes.

Miss Pine stepped forward to take a closer look. "Your mother's locket . . . Mrs. Wiggins told me . . . it's lovely."

"Would you help me put it on?" Annaliese asked her.

"But of course."

At last—at last!—Olivia's long-lost locket had found a loving home.

If Throckmorton could have, he would have pinned a medal on Evan's chest.

Moments later, Annaliese stretched on tiptoe to peer over the stair railing. Miss Pine and Mrs. Wiggins scurried down the elegantly decorated center hall staircase to take up their posts.

Easterlings from far and near surged into the two-story foyer below, greeted by chamber music played by a string quartet. A distinguished-looking valet took their coats and wraps. Miss Pine assisted by holding on to their sock monkeys while the keepers got settled.

Most of the guests were dressed in costumes: outlandish, exotic, elegant, absurd. Throckmorton spied wigs with towers of white curls and others with long black strings of hair. Sparkling with glitter, masks as beautiful as butterflies concealed partygoers' eyes.

Sadly, Throckmorton observed how the keepers' extravagant display upstaged the guests of honor: the sock monkeys.

Selfishly, perhaps, Throckmorton had envisioned an evening when human worries about wealth and status were cast aside to honor creatures as simple as he.

After all, wasn't that what Great-Grandmama had intended?

Annaliese and Throckmorton made their way down the wide carpeted stairs, one cautious step at a time. Judge Easterling waited near the bottom stair. He was dressed in a gray three-piece suit. Tucked in his arm, Miss Beatrice displayed the distinctive plaid of the Easterling clan.

As Throckmorton and Annaliese passed under a heart-shaped arch adorned with scarlet red roses, her father looked up.

His face fell.

Aunt Prudence, who stood next to the judge, lifted the mask off her face. "Oh my goodness!" she exclaimed.

A strange dreadful hush fell over the foyer.

"Why, Ellis," said the judge's oldest sister, loudly. "The child looks just like her mother."

The judge's eyes landed on the locket. For a moment, they brittled like ice.

Tightening her grip, Annaliese thrust Throckmorton out like a shield, as if Cupid and his arrows could prevent her father from stealing her joy.

"Annaliese, I've told you before: You are not to wear things that belong to—I mean—clothes that don't belong to . . ."

Annaliese's fingers flew to her locket, where they hovered like a mother bird protecting her young. "I know Father, but . . ."

Miss Pine moved to the judge's side. She tugged at his coat sleeve, urging him without words to back down. Teddy, disguised as a swashbuckling buccaneer, and Evan, in a Sherlock Holmes costume, took up positions next to Annaliese.

Suddenly, with a swish of her purple cape and a

wave of a sparkly wand, Aunt Pansy swooped into the space between her brother and his children.

"Great-Grandmama has arrived!" she shouted, drawing all attentions to herself. "The Grand March is about to begin."

Throckmorton didn't know what a Grand March was, but it did sound ever-so-special. And given that Judge Easterling was about to spoil the party, the timing was ever-so-handy.

"Remember," Aunt Pansy called out, "sock monkeys and their keepers only. Youngest to oldest!"

"Throckmorton," Annaliese gasped. "We're going to lead the Grand March!"

Throckmorton felt a swoon coming on . . . he could hardly believe his good fortune.

Aunt Pansy shoved a sheaf of papers into Miss Pine's hand. "If you don't know where you belong," she shouted, "ask Miss Pine."

As the sock monkeys and their keepers jostled for position, a bagpiper—Great-Grandmama's son Angus—burst forth, playing the first notes of a sour song. The other guests—spouses who weren't part of the Easterling bloodline—moved off to the side. The judge had no choice but to find a place near the middle of the line.

"Annaliese," her aunt hissed. "You're the youngest."

"What am I supposed to do?" Annaliese asked.

"Follow the piper."

Aunt Pansy's eyes narrowed. She lifted the locket off Annaliese's chest and examined the jeweled pendant more closely.

"Oh, you poor motherless child . . . ," she murmured, shaking her head.

"I'm not a motherless child," Annaliese confidently replied.

Turning Annaliese in the right direction, Aunt Pansy's elbow struck Throckmorton, bumping Cupid's quiver. A few of his pencil-arrows fell to the floor. Leaning over to pick them up, Annaliese mangled his left wing.

Just then, the trio of jungle cats—Nora, Nadine, and Nell Ann—squeezed into the line between Annaliese and Evan. The lioness, tigress, and leopardess clutched sock monkeys that were cloaked with fur—golden, striped, and spotted. Whiskers adorned the phony sock monkeys' faces.

"Nice costume, Annaliese," said Nadine snidely. "Love your monkey."

Aunt Pansy tapped her wand on the keepers' backs to keep them moving.

"Like lambs being led to the slaughter," Evan remarked.

On the third floor, a man in a black tuxedo opened the set of double doors that led into the ballroom.

Oh my, Throckmorton sighed as he drank in the splendor.

Golden moons, tulle angels, and glittery red horses with wings dangled through the folds of the draped ceiling. Thousands of velvet hearts on silver strings rained down from glistening chandeliers. Fresh pine boughs and wide lace ribbons with bows framed the windows. Candlelight set the stained glass ceiling dome aglow.

Three rings of linen-covered tables circled the dance floor. In the first ring, sock-monkey-sized tables were set with sock-monkey-sized dinnerware, sock-monkey-sized cutlery, and sock-monkey-sized stemmed glasses. Candles burned in the branches of tiny crystal candelabras set on round mirrors in the center of each table.

Great-Grandmama sat in a rose-colored wing chair in the center of the stage. She wore an evening gown with slashed sleeves, which was made of the palest of pink organza.

Strings of pearls weighed down her neck. A circle of tiny mauve roses crowned her silver-white hair. Ebenezer the Lighthouse Keeper sat in her lap, unadorned.

The width and breadth of the plush armchair engulfed the Easterling family's matriarch. In spite of the power of her purse strings, she seemed diminished somehow, as if the ninety-year-old woman were an old-fashioned doll playing dress up.

The Grand March line snaked around the ballroom. Annaliese pointed at the large shiny letters printed across the stage skirt. "The Bird Land Big Band," she read aloud. "Starring Miss Chickadee Finch."

When all the guests filled the ballroom, a drum rolled.

The crowd hushed.

The leader of the band, who introduced himself as Joe Crane, joined Great-Grandmama onstage. Joe was dressed in a light blue suit with a skinny silver stripe down the side of his trousers.

The bandleader spoke into the microphone with a deep creamy-sounding voice. "Good evening, ladies and gentlemen, sock monkey boys and sock monkey girls. The moment you've all been waiting for: It's time for the birthday girl to greet her royal guests."

Steadied by her fox-head cane, Great-Grandmama Easterling rose out of her chair. Great-Grandmama's oldest son, George, came on stage and stood by her side.

Annaliese's great-uncle held the first sock monkey that Great-Grandmama had ever made. Named Miss Ida S. Monkey, her well-loved and under-stuffed body looked like a weary old sock with a threadbare smile. (If Miss Ida's heart hid a precious jewel, Throckmorton figured that Great-Uncle George would've found it by now.)

George leaned over and kissed his mother's powdered cheek, and the band burst into the Happy Birthday song.

Everyone sang along.

With a small and shaking hand, Great-Grandmama waved triumphantly. She smiled down on her beloved sock monkeys; each and every one smiled back.

The song that Throckmorton sang inside his heart wasn't loud, but it was strong.

How, on this most magical and marvelous of nights, could he not love and honor the woman who had brought him into being?

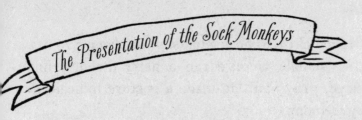

A trio of trumpet players sounded their horns. Ushers, looking like penguins in their black-and-white tuxedos, unrolled a long red carpet on the floor down the center of the ballroom.

Joe, the leader of the Bird Land Big Band, strutted to the center of the stage. He tapped a conductor's baton on the palm of his hand.

"Ladies and gentlemen, may I have your attention please? The Presentation of the Sock Monkeys is about to begin."

Great-Uncle George and Great-Grandmama approached the microphone stand together. The bandleader stepped aside. Ebenezer the Lighthouse Keeper remained onstage seated in Great-Grandmama's rose-colored wing chair.

Great-Uncle George placed Great-Grandmama's brown-leather ledger on a music stand. Then he adjusted the stand so that Great-Grandmama could easily read the names printed on the page.

"Keepers," stated Great-Uncle George with his characteristically dramatic flair, "when my mother calls your sock monkey's name, please step forward."

Great-Grandmama pulled on his coat sleeve. Her

son leaned close to hear what she was saying.

Great-Uncle George ran a hand through his shock of gray hair. He made a gesture indicating his agreement.

Speaking into the microphone, he delivered Great-Grandmama's edict: "Keepers, remove all masks, please. Shed your disguises. Only then may you present your sock monkey to its maker."

At once the ballroom was abuzz. Great-Grandmama waited impatiently while all the masks came off.

Evan nudged Annaliese. "Granny doesn't look too happy."

"I told you so."

Then Great-Grandmama slipped on a pair of reading glasses.

The tension in the ballroom was palpable as the crowd anticipated Great-Grandmama calling out the first name.

"Dame Lorraine S. Monkey," she announced, "accompanied by Mrs. Margaret Easterling, the wife of my son, the late John Easterling."

Annaliese, who had started to step forward, pulled back. "Oops! She's calling the older people first."

The band's pianist played a dignified march as the judge's arthritic mother, in a wheelchair proudly pushed by Mrs. Wiggins, made her way down the red carpet. Dame Lorraine, Margaret's bejeweled sock monkey, sat in her lap.

Next, Great-Uncle Angus and Miss Ernestine S. Monkey, who was costumed as a flapper in a peach drop-waist satin dress, came down the aisle. Great-Uncle Angus stopped in front of the stage, bowed, and blew his mother a kiss. Then he turned to face the crowd, holding the resplendent Miss Ernestine high over his head for all to see.

The spectacle was unlike anything Throckmorton had ever experienced. Never once had he imagined that such praise, adulation, and respect would be bestowed upon his own kind.

Pride penetrated every thread of Throckmorton's being.

Oldest to youngest, Great-Grandmama's descendants proceeded to present their sock monkeys.

After every bow or curtsy, the ever-observant Throckmorton noticed that Great-Grandmama raised either one finger or two. Every time she raised two fingers, Great-Uncle George nodded as though making a mental note.

Women in cream-colored silk suits seated the sock monkeys at the sock-monkey-sized tables set for four. Keepers took their places at larger tables set for eight.

Soon Great-Grandmama called out, "Miss Beatrice S. Monkey . . . accompanied by the Honorable Judge Ellis Easterling."

Annaliese leaned past the person in front of her to get a better look. Throckmorton couldn't see Miss Beatrice, but he did catch a glimpse of Miss Pine standing on the sidelines.

Miss Pine caught the judge's eye and smiled. Judge Easterling almost smiled back.

Throckmorton wasn't sure how he felt about this budding romance. For a long time, he'd held on to the hope that Olivia might return someday, that she and the judge would reconcile.

However, if Miss Pine—whom Annaliese seemed to like—could get the judge to collapse his black umbrella and see some sunshine in his life . . . why, that would be a most welcome change.

Oh, human love . . . it seemed so tedious and unnecessarily complicated.

"Sir Rudyard S. Monkey, accompanied by Evan Michael Easterling," Throckmorton now heard. This was followed by "Captain Eugene S. Monkey, accompanied by Theodore Vincent Easterling."

Decked out in a skull-and-crossbones hat, Teddy gripped spiffy Captain Eugene in one hand and a stuffed green parrot in the other.

Evan carried the always-debonair Sir Rudyard,

who he'd renamed Doctor Watson in honor of the occasion. Bailey the bloodhound was leashed at Evan's side. Evan, who was dressed in a houndstooth suit, puffed on an empty tobacco pipe. The magnifying glass "worthy of Sherlock Holmes" peeked out of his jacket pocket.

By this time, the ninety-year-old birthday girl appeared fatigued. Great-Uncle George took hold of her arm to help her stay upright.

Nearing the end of the procession, Nora, Nadine, and Nell Ann giggled their way up to the stage, curtsied, and skipped away. Grim-faced, Great-Grandmama held up two fingers for each one.

Throckmorton conclusively decoded what her finger signals meant.

Great-Grandmama wasn't half-blind, not by a long shot.

"And now, last but not least," she said hoarsely, "Mr. Throckmorton S. Monkey, accompanied by Annaliese Elizabeth Easterling."

The crowd silenced, all eyes focused on Annaliese and her sock monkey, a.k.a. Venus and Cupid.

Annaliese's lower lip trembled. Sweat from her palms seeped into Throckmorton's brown-and-cream skin. A few of his Cupid feathers fluttered to the floor.

Annaliese hesitated. For a teensy-tiny moment

she gazed into the mirror of Throckmorton's smiling face.

She took one step forward. Then she took another.

When they came to the end of the red carpet, Annaliese lifted her chin and held her head high. Great-Grandmama's face glowed with pride as she smiled down upon her youngest great-grandchild.

Throckmorton's and Ebenezer's eyes met.

Was Great-Grandmama telling the truth, he wondered. Would Annaliese *really* see her mother again?

Throckmorton didn't have the answers, but he certainly had his doubts.

Whew!"

Annaliese wiped the sweat off her brow with the back of her hand as soon as she came out of her curtsy.

One silk-suited usher whisked Throckmorton out of Annaliese's hands. A different usher escorted Annaliese to an outer ring of tables where the rest of Ethel Constance Easterling's great-grandchildren were already seated.

As he approached the sock-monkey-sized tables, Throckmorton realized how badly he wanted to sit next to Miss Beatrice.

Not that they'd be able to dine, drink fine wine, or dance cheek-to-cheek, but they could pretend— couldn't they?

When Throckmorton eyed the remaining sock-monkey-sized chair, his hopes were dashed.

Phooey, phooey, fiddlesticks!

Nora's, Nadine's, and Nell Ann's imposter sock monkeys occupied the other three chairs. Dressed up as jungle cat cubs, they stared at him with vacant, nonseeing eyes.

At times like this, Throckmorton truly wished that he could wrinkle his embroidered nose.

The usher set Throckmorton on a white cloth-covered chair decorated with a scarlet sash. She unfolded a linen napkin and laid it in Throckmorton's lap.

Waiters in tight white jackets now swept into the ballroom, balancing silver serving trays loaded with glass flutes.

Guests clinked glasses with silver spoons, calling for silence.

Great-Grandmama stood up. She placed her ringless hand on the back of the rose-colored chair to steady herself.

Great-Uncle George moved the microphone into place.

"My dear descendants," Great-Grandmama said, drawing her words out gradually, "thank you . . . from the bottom of my heart . . . for being here tonight to celebrate my ninetieth birthday."

"Thank you for . . ."

She paused. Her tear-filled eyes traveled across a sea of smiling sock monkey faces.

"For . . ."

Her voice broke. She swiped a few errant tears off her cheeks.

"For bringing my sock monkeys . . . home."

The keepers gave Great-Grandmama a heartfelt round of applause.

"Like me," she continued in a somber tone of voice after the clapping ceased, "some of you have compounded your fortunes. Others have gambled and lost. Still others are waiting—quite patiently, I might add—for me to die."

Throckmorton sensed a swell of discomfort wash over the crowd.

"When the clock strikes ten," Great-Grandmama said, "ninety candles will be lit and my birthday cake will be served. Shortly after, I will make an important announcement regarding my last will and testament.

"But for now, I leave you with one thought: Everything you need to live a rich and happy life already resides inside your sock monkey's heart. Love . . . and loyalty . . ."

Great-Grandmama's cane shook beneath her trembling hand. She moved her mouth away from the microphone as her voice trailed off.

Seated quite close to the stage, Throckmorton heard every word Great-Grandmama had said: "Love . . . and loyalty . . . listening . . . and a never-ending smile."

Later he'd discover that a number of humans

either hadn't been listening or heard only what they wanted to hear.

Great-Uncle George readjusted the microphone. Great-Grandmama pulled a handkerchief out from her under sash. "Oh, there I go, getting all weepy and preachy, which I promised myself I wouldn't do."

She lifted her glass flute to toast her descendants. "And so tonight, let us eat, drink, and be merry, for . . . soon . . ." She took a sip of the bubbly beverage. "I *will* die." Great-Grandmama chuckled. "I promise."

Following her shocking words, there was dead silence.

And then . . . an eruption of high-pitched chatter and nervous laughter.

Great-Uncle George guided Great-Grandmama and Ebenezer the Lighthouse Keeper to the head table. The glitzy Bird Land Big Band returned to the stage.

At the next table over, Throckmorton overheard Captain Eugene say to Miss Beatrice, "Well, we can't eat . . ."

"And we can't drink," added Sir Rudyard.

"But we can be merry," said Dame Lorraine joyfully.

The four sock monkeys chortled. The band burst

into a song with a bouncy beat. The sock monkeys, who were being ignored by their keepers, chit-chatted to their hearts' content.

Throckmorton couldn't eat.

He couldn't drink.

And he couldn't be merry.

Not when he was stuck sitting with three phony sock monkeys who had no sense at all.

Throckmorton could overhear Captain Eugene telling a lively sea-faring tale; Miss Beatrice was all ears. Dame Lorraine invited her to visit London. After that exchange, Sir Rudyard recited a love sonnet, as if he and Miss Beatrice were the only two sock monkeys in the room.

Jealousy, the lime-green kind, nibbled away at Throckmorton's insides.

Judge Easterling was right, he muttered; life is never fair.

But then something that Miss Beatrice had once said came to mind. "Perhaps," she'd suggested, "*all* stuffed animals are more like us than not. Perhaps they have their own special language—a language that we sock monkeys can neither hear nor understand."

Throckmorton's good manners came to the fore. He smiled the kind of smile that took a direct route from his heart.

"A pleasure to meet you," he said to Nell Ann's sock monkey.

Seconds passed.

No response.

More seconds passed.

Throckmorton's good will dried up quickly.

"A-hem!" A loud stern voice asserted itself.

Uh-oh . . . had a human overheard him speak?

Great-Uncle George and another man who was tall and wearing a dark suit towered above Throckmorton's table.

Great-Uncle George opened Great-Grandmama's ledger.

"*That*," he said, pointing at the sock monkey that Nora brought, "is not the authentic Adeline S. Monkey."

Great-Uncle George pointed a second time. "*That* is not the bona fide Minnie S. Monkey."

Great-Uncle George pointed a third time. "*That* is not the genuine Bartholomew S. Monkey."

With long bony fingers, the tall man plucked the three fraudulent sock monkeys out of their seats.

Soon, from other parts of the ballroom, wails of human protest rose:

"No! Please don't!"

"Wait! We can explain!"

"It's all a big misunderstanding!"

The purge of a total of eight sock monkey imposters was executed with haste. Their keepers—including Nora, Nadine, Nell Ann, and their parents—were shown the door.

Tables for human guests were quickly rearranged. And then the announcement: "Dinner is served."

No one seemed to notice that Throckmorton was dining solo. And if they had, no one seemed to care.

Trapped in a fishing net! he muttered.

Stranded in a snow bank! he sputtered.

And now, all alone at a party.

He was fed up!

Fed up with feeling helpless.

Tired of being left behind.

Wasn't there something—anything—he could do about it?

He was about to answer his own question—No!—when Annaliese materialized. She perched on the tiny chair next to him, Ebenezer in hand.

Now that her triplet cousins were gone, Throckmorton realized, there were no other girls Annaliese's age at the party.

"I can't wait any longer," she told him. "I have to talk to Great-Grandmama now! She *has* to tell me everything she knows about my mother."

She looked anxiously around the ballroom. "But I've looked everywhere and I can't find her."

Annaliese's tulle-and-lace cape hung crookedly.

The bottom of her gown had been trampled upon.

"I went to the head table. Great-Grandmama's chair was empty. And she had barely touched her food. I asked, but no one would tell me where she or Great-Uncle George had gone. Then I saw Ebenezer lying all alone on the floor."

With both hands, she squeezed Ebenezer's chest, as if proving to herself that the diamond remained inside.

"I hate secrets!" she blurted.

She peered into Throckmorton's eyes. "Maybe I should tell Teddy. What do you think?"

Don't tell anyone!

That's what Throckmorton thought.

"Now that Father is home," she said glumly, "who knows when I'll get to visit Great-Grandmama again. Tonight may be my only chance."

Throckmorton wished that Annaliese would stop talking this way.

She'd made a promise.

When the time was right, Great-Grandmama would tell her everything she needed to know.

At that very moment, Evan, Teddy, and a few of their older boy cousins sauntered up to the table.

"What's wrong with you?" Evan asked Annaliese. "It's a party. You're supposed to be having fun."

He handed her a small glass cup filled with

punch. "Here, drink this. It'll cheer you up."

Annaliese took a sip, made a face, and gave it back. "I don't like it. It tastes funny. What's in it?"

"Punch." Evan smirked. "With a punch."

The boys laughed.

"Annaliese has a secret," Evan announced. "Or so she says."

"I do have a secret," she replied.

"Come on, you can tell us." Evan glanced at the crowded dance floor. "If you do, Teddy will dance with you. Won't you, Teddy?"

Teddy's face reddened. He shrugged as if he had no choice in the matter.

Annaliese seemed to be considering the offer.

Don't! Throckmorton protested.

This is not the time! This is not the place!

Why, the very idea positively curdled his stuffing.

Evan pulled Ebenezer out of his sister's lap. He set the sock monkey on the little chair next to Throckmorton's.

"You don't have to sit here all by yourself." Evan tugged on Annaliese's arm. "Come on, you can hang out with us for a while."

"Oh, all right," said Annaliese reluctantly. "Stay here, Ebenezer—and you too, Throckmorton. Don't move. I'll be back soon."

Throckmorton was dying to ask Ebenezer if he

knew what had happened to Great-Grandmama. But before the sock monkeys had a chance to speak, the flashy bandleader stepped up to the microphone.

"And now, ladies and gentlemen . . . about to begin her first North American tour . . . the amazing, the incredible, Miss Chickadee Finch!"

At first, the appearance of a soloist named after a small insignificant bird didn't seem to impress the crowd. As she stole out of the shadows to take center stage, most people kept talking loudly amongst themselves.

Then, the spotlight found her.

Miss Chickadee Finch wore a sleek silver-gray tuxedo with feathered coat tails. Tied over her white shirt was a small black bib. Her black cap sported a pointy brim. The cap extended just over her nose, making her eyes appear dark and beady.

Her hair was hidden from view. Her cheeks were whitened and lips painted persimmon orange. Tight gray gloves made her fingers look like claws.

Odd, but enchanting, Throckmorton decided.

Given the approving hush that descended upon the ballroom, the human beings must have agreed.

Slightly behind and off to Miss Finch's side, a violinist tucked his instrument under his chin and laid a bow on its strings. The pianist played a few

bars of introduction. On the downbeat, Miss Finch sang the first words of her first song.

Her voice wove up, down, and around the ballroom, as if casting a spell. The lonely, almost holy sound of the violin wound like a ribbon around her words, slow and haunting.

As Throckmorton listened to the dreamy beat of songs that were filled with love and longing and loss, the yellow duck diaper pin seemed to be digging deeper and deeper into his chest.

The songs were foreign to Throckmorton's ear, and yet the longer he listened, the more familiar the singer's voice sounded.

The final song of Miss Finch's set had a weeping melody with a sad refrain.

Before he knew it, Throckmorton was singing to himself: *Sock-monkey, Throck-monkey . . . rock-around-the-clock-monkey . . .*

In his mind, he traveled back in time to Annaliese's cradle. He saw himself smiling down on Olivia's brand-new baby girl.

Throckmorton's suspicions grew stronger.

The singer's voice . . . that tune . . . the clever disguise . . .

Was it possible?

After almost nine years of absence, would Olivia dare to crash Great-Grandmama's ninetieth birthday party? And if she had, what would happen if the judge found out?

Throckmorton shuddered, recalling Captain Eugene's description of Judge Easterling's anger the night he discovered his young wife, suitcase in hand, saying good-bye to her sons.

The dancers glided past . . . Aunt Pansy and Uncle Ray . . . Judge Easterling and Aunt Penelope . . . Max and Mrs. Wiggins . . . people who'd known Olivia well.

They showed no signs of recognition.

If Throckmorton could see past Olivia's disguise, why couldn't they?

Maybe he was mistaken . . .

He certainly hoped so. Tonight didn't seem to be the right time or the right place for a mother and child reunion.

Finally, Throckmorton located Annaliese. She and Teddy stood in the middle of the dance floor, shifting their feet back and forth, an arm's length apart. Annaliese talked and Teddy listened.

Had Annaliese traded her secret for a silly and insignificant dance?

Ignorant of the diamond hidden inside his heart, Ebenezer kept smiling his crooked smile.

Meanwhile, Throckmorton's heart filled with fear and uncertainty.

He should be having fun. It was a sock monkey ball after all—the first, and perhaps only, of his life.

But no matter how hard he tried, he couldn't shake the feeling that disaster was heading this way.

Miss Chickadee Finch left the stage following an outburst of unrestrained applause. The younger members of the Easterling family, impressed but lulled by her haunting ballads, demanded that the Bird Land Big Band liven things up.

"Play some swing!" Cousin Willie shouted.

Couples crowded the floor, dancing to the beat, kicking up their feet. Chair-bound, Throckmorton envied the ease with which they moved.

If only he could rise, stroll over to the next table and ask Miss Beatrice to dance. He'd whirl her and twirl her until she was spinning and brimming with delight.

Now that would be fun!

So what if she was a few decades older than he?

Why should age matter?

Opposites attract—isn't that what Miss Beatrice said?

Throckmorton's mind was just getting into the swing of things when Ebenezer the Lighthouse Keeper rudely interrupted his reveries.

"Something funny is going on," the sock monkey asserted.

"What do you mean?" Throckmorton inquired.

"Earlier backstage," Ebenezer started to explain, "Great-Grandmama was talking to the singer."

The singer?

Why would Great-Grandmama be speaking with the singer? Unless . . .

"There's nothing strange about that," Throckmorton replied, reluctant to reveal his suspicions. "I think Miss Finch has an awfully good voice."

"Actually," Ebenezer said, "they were arguing."

"Arguing? About what?"

Word for word, Ebenezer related the conversation between Great-Grandmama and Miss Chickadee Finch:

"You promised," Great-Grandmama reminded the singer.

"I know I did," she answered.

"And I promised that I'd let you see them. Not speak to them."

"I know, I know."

"It's too soon," Great-Grandmama said. *"You can't walk back into their lives as if you've never been gone."*

Ebenezer described how the singer pressed her hands over her face.

"But now that I've seen them . . . they're—they're—almost grown."

"What did you expect?" Great-Grandmama asked. *"Time doesn't stand still. Never has. Never will."* She clucked her tongue. *"For heaven's sake, Olivia, I assumed that by now you'd have gotten your head out of the clouds."*

"Wait! Back up," Throckmorton demanded. "Great-Grandmama called her Olivia? Are you positive?"

"Absolutely," Ebenezer answered. "Why?"

Throckmorton shook off the urge to explain. "Never mind—go on. I interrupted you."

Ebenezer continued:

"Nobody would like to see you reunited with those children more than I," Great-Grandmama said. *"But not here. Not now. Sing your songs and be on your way."*

"Please . . ."

"You've waited nine years; you can wait a little longer. I'll decide when it's time to take the next step."

Throckmorton replayed the scene in his mind.

Poor Annaliese . . .

His sweet keeper was trapped between a schemer and a dreamer; a sticky web of deceit from which she might never break free.

"And then what happened?" he asked Ebenezer.

"Great-Grandmama asked Great-Uncle George to bring around a wheelchair; she was feeling a little faint."

"And . . . ?"

"He did," said Ebenezer. "Great-Uncle George gave us a ride to the head table. After Great-Grandmama ate a spoonful of soup, she said that she felt dizzy."

Ebenezer imitated Great-Grandmama's tone of voice perfectly: *"The excitement . . . too much excitement . . . I'm so warm . . . I need a little air . . ."*

"So," Ebenezer said, "Great-Uncle George removed her shawl and I accidentally tumbled off her lap. He either didn't notice or didn't care, and then he wheeled her away."

"Is Great-Grandmama sick?"

"I don't know . . . maybe," Ebenezer admitted. "I mean, she was. The doctor stopped by the carriage house a couple of times earlier this week."

Throckmorton thought about secrets.

He thought about silence.

Didn't Ebenezer have the right to know the truth about how he came into being and why?

Throckmorton answered his own question: Yes!

"Something funny *is* going on . . . ," he told Ebenezer.

Quickly, lest Annaliese return and interrupt their conversation, Throckmorton explained the three basic truths about Ebenezer's existence.

One: Annaliese was his maker.

Two: He had a priceless diamond tucked inside his red felt heart.

Three: After Great-Grandmama died, Ebenezer was to be given to Annaliese's mother, Olivia, a.k.a. Miss Chickadee Finch.

Ebenezer looked at him with stunned, staring eyes. "But—but—why?" he stammered.

"To make amends, I guess."

Throckmorton repeated what he'd heard Great-Grandmama tell Annaliese: *"We Easterlings treated her badly. I've never forgiven myself."*

"She must feel guilty," Throckmorton concluded.

"I guess I'm not surprised," Ebenezer said after a prolonged silence. "About the diamond, I mean. My heart feels awfully heavy. The diamond must be huge."

"Oh, that it is," Throckmorton confirmed.

"Thanks for telling me, Throckmorton. Ever since this party began, I've been feeling out of place—like I don't belong. You know—like I'm not a *real* Easterling. Now I understand why." Ebenezer sighed. "And about Olivia one day becoming my keeper . . . um, I don't know how I feel about that," he said. "In some ways, it's kind of an honor."

An honor?

Throckmorton had never considered Ebenezer's creation in that light. "What do you mean?"

"I guess I'm here to give Annaliese hope."

Throckmorton's desire to do something truly remarkable someday paled in comparison to Ebenezer's lofty purpose. If any red-heeled sock monkey was destined to become unforgettable, it was Ebenezer.

Weighed down by his sudden insight, Throckmorton's own heart felt like an anchor about to sink to the bottom of the sea.

The Bird Land Big Band took a break. The dancers, red faced and perspiring, headed for the punch bowl.

Whatever they were smiling about, Throckmorton didn't want to see. Whatever they were laughing about, he didn't want to hear.

He wanted Annaliese to come back—*now!*

That's all he wanted; his yearning was like a terrible thirst.

Suddenly, an unfamiliar finger hooked Throckmorton's ear.

A split second later, a woman (who he realized was Annaliese's Aunt Prudence) pulled the chair out from under him. Suspended in air, Throckmorton watched one of Cupid's tulle wings fall to the floor.

Aunt Prudence marched across the empty dance floor and set the small chair, with Throckmorton in it, against the wall. From the sidelines, he watched with disbelief as, one by one, the sock-monkey-sized tables were cleared, dismantled, and carried away.

Soon, a single row of forty-one sock monkeys lined the far wall. Apparently the dancers wanted more room to dance. The sock monkeys were in the way.

Fortunately, Throckmorton, Ebenezer, and Miss Beatrice were set upright in chairs right next to one another.

Other sock monkeys were less fortunate. Sir Rudyard lay on his back, splayed across Dame Lorraine's lap. Captain Eugene's face was wedged between his knees. His captain's hat and Dame Lorraine's mink stole had fallen to the floor.

"Look over there," said Miss Beatrice sadly.

Piled in the corner were the eight phony sock monkeys, ditched by their thoughtless keepers. Now

Throckmorton wished that he'd been a little nicer to his former tablemates.

A short while later, Aunt Priscilla and Aunt Pansy walked past.

"I'm afraid this party is getting a little out of hand," Aunt Priscilla complained.

Aunt Pansy flashed a cold smile at a loud bunch gathered around the punch bowl. "Those Midwesterners—they're not as dull as I thought."

Meanwhile, up and down the long row of sock monkeys, their anger gathered like thunder clouds before a storm.

Throckmorton's wrath was the first to erupt. "Where's Great-Grandmama?" he shouted. "I demand to know why we're being treated like—like—second fiddles!"

"Shush," cautioned Miss Beatrice. "The humans might hear you!"

"I don't care!" he shouted even more loudly.

"We're the guests of honor!" Dame Lorraine shrieked at the dancers. "You wouldn't even be here if it weren't for us."

Bolstered by his cousins' bravery, Captain Eugene cursed the mortals. "Avast! Ye scallywags! Ye scurvy dogs!"

But alas, no matter how bitterly the sock monkeys mumbled or how loudly they grumbled, their voices weren't heard. All their years of silence in the presence of humans had been unnecessary.

Throckmorton was at the end of his rope.

Why should hand-sewn sock monkeys listen to keepers who never listened to them?

Time crept on.

Planted like wallflowers, the sock monkeys watched and waited.

Sometime later, a woman wearing a white chef's hat rolled a large serving cart with wheels onto the stage. On the cart stood a monstrous, majestic three-tier cake, dotted with candles and decorated with swells of white frosting, red hearts, and pink roses.

Great-Grandmama's descendants surged toward the stage.

The band played the first few bars of the Happy Birthday song, hoping to coax the ninety-year-old birthday girl to come forward.

But Great-Grandmama failed to appear.

"Throckmorton, there's no other explanation. Something's happened to her," said Miss Beatrice. "I'm really quite worried."

Throckmorton agreed.

Something *had* happened.

Something bad.

Rumors skipped up and down Sock Monkey Row: *I saw Uncle Fred spike the punch . . . No, I saw Aunt Prudence spike the punch . . . No, it was Cousin Willy . . . Great-Grandmama must have drunk too much punch . . . Uncle Ray put poison in the punch . . .* and so on and so forth.

Evan and two of his cousins appeared now and filled the space right in front of Throckmorton's face.

"I'm not kidding," Evan asserted, too loud for Throckmorton not to hear. "That's what Annaliese told Teddy."

"I don't believe you," said the taller of the two cousins.

"She saw the diamond with her own eyes," Evan insisted. "It was huge!" He moved his finger up, down, and across his breastbone. "Cross my heart and hope to die."

Throckmorton's heart raced.

Annaliese must have spilled the secret about the diamond she'd placed in Ebenezer's heart. Had she also confessed that their mother, Olivia, was intended to receive Ebenezer?

Throckmorton strained to hear more.

"Evan could be right," said the shorter cousin. "Didn't you hear what Great-Grandmama said? The sock monkeys are going to make us rich!"

Evan smirked. "See . . . that's what I've been telling you."

The human cousins exchanged conspiratorial glances.

With arms spread across one another's shoulders, the three boys headed back to the punch bowl.

"Wait until I tell my dad," the tall boy told Evan.

"You'd better not," Evan warned. "Remember: It's a secret."

The Rightful Owner

The ninety candles on Ethel Constance Easterling's birthday cake were never lit. The uncut cake was pushed on its serving cart to the side of the stage. Joe Crane, the bandleader, picked up his baton and kicked off the next set. Only one couple drifted onto the dance floor.

Great-Grandmama's descendants milled restlessly about the ballroom. Their faces displayed a broad palette of feelings: foreheads etched with worry lines, cheeks flushed with frustration, painted smiles turned upside down.

Throckmorton could see Annaliese now as she reentered the ballroom. She surveyed the new arrangement of dining tables. Her eyes shifted.

When she caught sight of Throckmorton and Ebenezer, she made a beeline for their chairs along the side wall. She spoke to them with quiet urgency. "I found out what's happened. . . . Father said that I'm to 'keep it under wraps.'"

She picked up Throckmorton and tucked him under her left arm. Then she grabbed Ebenezer with her right hand. "She's going to need her sock monkey—let's go!"

Throckmorton heard Annaliese's wildly beating heart. Yet, as she moved through the crowd, her pace was slow but deliberate. "Excuse me, Aunt Patricia," she said politely. "Pardon me, Cousin Willie."

Once outside the ballroom, she broke into a run. Her ballet slippers skipped almost soundlessly down the well-worn wooden steps of the servants' staircase. On the first floor, rather than turning left toward the kitchen, she took a quick right. She dashed down a long carpeted hallway and cut through the portrait gallery with great haste.

Without warning, Judge Easterling burst through the doors of the library. He and Annaliese collided. Throckmorton's head twisted violently sideways. His shoulder collapsed. Cupid's second wing and his quiver slipped off. The remaining arrows scattered across the mosaic tile floor.

Annaliese didn't fall down, but she did have trouble catching her breath—a grim reminder that her recovery from the ill effects of pneumonia was far from complete.

"Is she still . . . still . . . ?" she asked her father.

"She's with Dr. Webb and Uncle George, near the side entrance around back," he said in a tender tone of voice that Throckmorton had rarely—if ever—heard him use before. "The ambulance should be here any minute. No sirens, I told them on the phone. No use getting everyone all riled up."

"Where are you going?" she asked.

"Back to the ballroom," the judge replied. "Everyone's waiting for Great-Grandmama's special announcement. I'd better tell them straight-out what happened. Nip any rumors in the bud. As far as I'm concerned, this party is over."

In a small hallway, Great-Grandmama lay on a wood-and-canvas cot, covered with a blanket. Great-Uncle George knelt beside her and held his mother's hands in his own.

"Do you know what's wrong? Is she going to be okay?" Annaliese asked the doctor.

"She may have suffered a stroke," Dr. Webb replied. "At first, I thought she'd had a heart attack, but . . ."

Dr. Webb put a stethoscope to her chest and listened to her heart.

A few moments later, he stood up and stretched out his back. "More likely than not, it's the party . . . the worry, the strain, a shock of some kind—it's too much for a woman of her age."

"Do—do you mean," Annaliese stammered, "like maybe something happened that upset her?"

"Quite possibly," the doctor said.

Annaliese pulled Throckmorton to her chest and dropped her chin. "Oh no!" she moaned.

"One way or the other, she's going to the hospital," Dr. Webb said. "We can't take any chances."

Annaliese took a few steps closer to the cot. "Great-Grandmama, it's me—Annaliese."

Great-Grandmama opened her eyes. Her face was grayish in color. All but one of the sweetheart roses had fallen out of her flower crown.

When she spoke, Great-Grandmama's voice was a ragged whisper. "No hospital."

Annaliese bent over her. "I brought your sock monkey. Ebenezer can go with you. He'll help you get well."

"Horses," she said. "Go home."

"What did she say?" asked Great-Uncle George.

"She doesn't want to go to the hospital," Annaliese answered. "She wants the horses to take her home."

Great-Uncle George rubbed his temples. "A sleigh ride? Why, that'll never do . . ."

Annaliese held Ebenezer out in front of Great-Grandmama. "See. It's Ebenezer the Lighthouse Keeper."

"Not now, Annaliese," Great-Uncle George admonished.

Great-Grandmama tilted her chin upward.

"Here. Take him." Annaliese lifted the blanket and laid Ebenezer across her chest.

"No, child." Great-Grandmama shook her head

ever-so-slightly. Suddenly, flashes of red light pulsed against the frosted window pane. Annaliese dashed to the back door. She scratched on the icy glass until there was a clear patch. "It's the ambulance!"

Dr. Webb flung open the door. Two men and a woman in dark blue jackets burst inside and set a stretcher down next to the cot.

Great-Grandmama's eyes filled with terror. "Sock . . . monkey . . . ," she rasped.

"No! Wait!" Annaliese cried. "She's trying to tell me something."

Annaliese dropped to her knees beside the cot. Dr. Webb held up his hand, and the emergency people paused.

"Be . . . longs . . . to . . . ," said Great-Grandmama, slurring her words.

"I know who Ebenezer belongs to," Annaliese assured her. "I won't forget—I promise. But *you* need him now."

"Belongs to . . ." Great-Grandmama's parched lips looked as if they might crumble if she spoke one more word. "Misssss . . ."

Great-Uncle George gripped Annaliese, but she shook him off.

"Ch—Ch—" The word stuck in Great-Grandmama's throat.

"She's getting cold, Annaliese. It's time to go," said Dr. Webb.

"What are you trying to say?" Annaliese asked one more time.

"Sssss . . ."

Steadily, like a church bell tolling in his heart, Throckmorton chanted the two syllables of the yet unspoken word: *sing-er . . . sing-er . . . sing-er . . .*

"Ss—ss—singer," Great-Grandmama gasped with what Throckmorton feared was her last breath.

Uncertainty washed across Annaliese's face.

"Annaliese, she's confused," said Dr. Webb. "Tell her that you understand, even if you don't."

Annaliese pressed her lips on Great-Grandmama's cheek. "Don't worry . . . I understand."

The doctor pressed his thumb on Great-Grandmama's wrist to check her pulse.

Annaliese's sweaty hands squeezed Throckmorton's arms. "Is she—is she—?"

"It's steady."

Great-Uncle George heaved a sigh of relief. He wiped his eyes and blew his nose into a crumpled white handkerchief.

When Dr. Webb gave the go-ahead, the rescue workers shifted Great-Grandmama onto the stretcher. Ebenezer glided off Great-Grandmama's chest. Annaliese tried to hand Ebenezer back to her, but Great-Uncle George shook his head.

"A hospital is no place for a sock monkey. What if he gets lost?"

Great-Uncle George drew the sock monkey out of Annaliese's hand and then dropped Ebenezer onto the empty cot.

Ebenezer landed face-up. With one arm extended above his head, he appeared to be reaching for the crushed sweetheart rose that had fallen out of Great-Grandmama's hair.

Great-Uncle George and Dr. Webb buttoned up their coats and followed the stretcher out the door. Before the doctor left, he looked back over his shoulder. "Go on now, Annaliese—back to the party."

As the ambulance sped off, Annaliese stood with her forehead pressed against the window's cold glass.

Hanging in her hand, Throckmorton readied himself for Annaliese's mad dash back to the ballroom.

She'd made the connection, hadn't she?

She must have, Throckmorton figured.

After all, Great-Grandmama had told her exactly what she needed to know: Ebenezer the Lighthouse Keeper belongs to the singer. Miss Chickadee Finch is a singer. Therefore, Miss Chickadee Finch is her mother.

Logic. Pure and simple.

Annaliese collapsed onto a chair next to an empty umbrella stand. "I don't know what to do," she whispered.

From somewhere down the hall a clock announced the half hour.

Bong!

Annaliese raised Throckmorton's body until they were eye-to-eye. Her face looked chalky. Her voice was shaky.

"Oh, Throckmorton, everything's gone wrong . . . I broke my promise, and told Teddy about the diamond inside Ebenezer's heart, and Great-Grandmama is so sick, and maybe she'll die, and then I told her that I understood what she was trying to tell me, but I didn't . . . I didn't understand at all!"

Now the bridge of Annaliese's nose beaded with sweat. "I don't feel so well," she said almost breathlessly.

She leaned her head against the back of the chair. Her arms went limp. Her fingers spread.

Throckmorton's body dropped headfirst into the umbrella stand.

Doggone it all anyway!

His legs dangled over the edge of the stand, catching his fall. His smile was hidden from view.

In this miserable position, how was he supposed

to comfort the little girl whom he loved?

Time passed. How much, he didn't know.

Throckmorton could do nothing but wait.

Had Annaliese fainted?

Had she fallen asleep?

Why hadn't anyone—the judge or her brothers or Miss Pine—come looking for her?

Throckmorton thought back on those long, lonely months when he'd been trapped in the fishy-smelling net. He recalled how badly he'd desired some kind of assurance that he'd never be forgotten about again.

But now, in the deepest reaches of his heart, Throckmorton knew that he'd give up every one of his impossible dreams if only Annaliese could be reunited with her mother.

And if that meant he'd have to spend the rest of his days like this, or with store-bought stuffed animals that had no sense at all, so be it.

Bong . . . Bong . . . Bong . . .

The clock's midnight tolling sounded like a death knell.

With the clock's final *Bong!* still echoing in his ears, Throckmorton heard Ebenezer the Lighthouse Keeper start to speak. His cousin's voice was that of a wise and seasoned storyteller.

Ebenezer was talking about a lost bird who

couldn't find her way back home. One night, the bird, a black-capped chickadee, found herself battered by the raging winds of a terrible storm at sea. Terrified and about to give up hope, she spied at last the blinking beams of a lighthouse's brightly burning beacon.

The ever-watchful lighthouse keeper saw the chickadee's distress and took pity on her. He drew open the lighthouse window, stretched out his rain-splashed hand, and offered the lost bird a safe, albeit slippery, place to land.

Throckmorton would be the last sock monkey to say that Annaliese had heard even one word of what Ebenezer was saying.

And yet, all of a sudden, Annaliese sprang into action.

She yanked Throckmorton out of the umbrella stand, grabbed Ebenezer by the arm, and took off running.

"Miss Chickadee Finch! The singer!" she cried. "Ebenezer belongs to the singer!"

U p and down the hallway, not a soul was in sight. The ballroom was locked.

"What's going on?" Annaliese cried out, pounding on the stubborn double doors. "Where did everybody go?"

She tucked Throckmorton and Ebenezer under the same arm and raced down a dimly lit passageway that led to the rear of the stage. The back door into the ballroom was wide open.

Throckmorton heard no voices, no laughter, no music.

"I'm too late! The party's over."

Annaliese stepped into the unlit, empty ballroom. Shafts of moonlight cut through the stained-glass dome, creating a kaleidoscope of eerily colored shadows. The candelabra candles had been snuffed out, yet the air still smelled smoky. The *Starring Miss Chickadee Finch* stage sign lay crumpled on the floor.

"She's gone," Annaliese whispered. "I missed my chance . . . my only chance."

Now, footsteps sounded on the stage.

Out of the darkness a man's voice called, "Hello? Is anybody still here?"

Annaliese froze.

"Hello?" he called again.

"There's nobody here," she shouted back, "except me."

"It's Joe, from the Bird Land Big Band. In the rush to get out of here, I dropped my baton. One of my guys—Bud, the fiddler—left his violin case. I came back to get them."

"Rush? What rush?" Annaliese asked herself out loud.

Onstage, the bandleader's silhouette took shape. Cautiously he stepped closer to its edge. "You don't by any chance know how to turn on the footlights, do you?"

"No, I don't."

The bandleader fumbled about on the dark stage.

"Hey, I found them!" he said. "Thanks. I'll be on my way. Sorry to have bothered you."

"Wait! Don't go!" she cried.

Annaliese dashed up the short flight of stage stairs. On the top step, she tripped on her costume's gold cord. She spread her fingers to break her fall. Throckmorton and Ebenezer went flying in different directions. Her knees smacked against the floor.

Joe ran to her side. "Are you all right? Here, let me give you a hand."

Setting the violin case close to where Throck-morton had landed, he hoisted Annaliese to her feet.

"Where's the singer?" she asked in a panicked voice. "Miss Finch. I have to speak with her."

"Long gone, little girl," Joe answered. "She didn't stick around for her last set. She lost her voice, or so she said."

"Do you know where she went?"

"One of guys drove her back to the hotel."

"What hotel?"

"Why do you ask?"

"I told you. It's important."

"Listen," Joe said, taking a few steps back, "I've got to get going."

"Please, sir," Annaliese begged, "will you give something to her?"

"Maybe . . . I can't make any promises. What is it?"

Annaliese scooped Ebenezer and Throckmorton off the floor.

Throckmorton knew at once that something was amiss. Annaliese had tucked him into the crook of her right arm. She'd tucked Ebenezer into the crook of her left arm—where Throckmorton belonged—in his favorite spot, right next to her heart.

"It's a sock monkey," she told Joe. "Tell Miss Finch that it's a gift from . . . um, uh, from Great-Grandmama Easterling."

Joe scoffed. "Gosh darn, you people and your sock monkeys . . . I don't get it." He shook his head. "This was the craziest party we've ever played, by a long shot."

"Please . . . ," Annaliese appealed again.

"Sure, why not." Joe flipped open the empty violin case. "Throw it in here. The last thing I need is for one of the guys to see me hanging around with a stuffed monkey. I'd never hear the end of it."

Annaliese's fingers clasped Throckmorton's neck.

Stop! he cried.

You've got the wrong monkey!

Too late.

The lid closed, latches clicked, and the last flickers of light extinguished. Inside the violin case, Throckmorton's limbs contorted. His tail roped his neck like a noose. The velvety lining tickled his nose.

The case started to swing back and forth, back and forth like a pendulum.

Throckmorton sickened with fear.

Joe didn't seem like the type of guy who had a soft spot in his heart for stuffed animals.

If only Annaliese would realize her mistake before it's too late . . .

Ker-plunk! The violin case made a hard landing.

A moment later, an automobile engine sputtered, rumbled, and started to purr.

As the car drove off, Throckmorton faced a brutal truth: A red-heeled sock monkey is, was, and always will be just one human whim away from slipping out of sight forever.

Alas, Great-Grandmama's not-so-grand birthday party had taken its toll. Entombed and exhausted, Throckmorton entered into a troubled slumber.

No Turning Back

Throckmorton awoke with a start.

He didn't know where he was, who he was with, or how long he'd been sleeping.

There was a rap on wood and the clink of a chain.

"Joe!" he heard a woman say. "What are you doing here?"

Throckmorton recognized the voice: Olivia!

Praise be . . . the bandleader had kept his word.

"I've got something for you," Joe said. "Special delivery."

"Now?" Olivia asked. "Can't it wait until morning? I'm trying to get some sleep."

"It's from a little girl at that party," Joe explained. "I ran into her backstage. I'd driven back to get my baton and the violin case that Bud left behind."

"The pretty one in the long white dress?"

"Yeah," Joe answered. "The girl with the straggly hair."

"Come on in," Olivia urged.

"She seemed pretty upset."

"What is it?"

The violin case tilted upright and the lid swung open. "See for yourself."

When Throckmorton's eyes adjusted, Olivia's face came into focus, haloed by bronze light. Her eyes were puffy. Smudges of makeup marked her face. And her hair! It was cut as short as Evan's.

With one of her long painted fingernails, Olivia tapped his yellow duck diaper pin. "It's Throckmorton!"

Joe gave his forehead a soft blow with the back of his hand. "Don't tell me you know this guy!"

Olivia drew Throckmorton out of the case. "Tell me exactly what the girl said."

For a split second, Joe hesitated.

"Tell me!" she demanded.

"Like I said, I bumped into her backstage. She startled me—I wasn't expecting anyone to be back there. It was dark and she tripped."

"Did she get hurt?"

"Nah, I don't think so," Joe said. "I helped her up and she seemed fine. Anyway, she had two sock monkeys. She shoved this one into my arms and made me promise that I'd give it to you." He paused. "Like I said, she was really upset."

Olivia looked deeply into Throckmorton's black button eyes. "Why would she want me to have her sock monkey?"

Joe gripped the doorknob. "Oh, I forgot . . . she told me to tell you that it was a present from Great-

Grandmama. You know, the old lady who hired us."

Olivia turned Throckmorton upside down and right side up, examining every inch of his body. "Nothing else?" she asked Joe. "No note or anything?"

"Nope." Joe threw up his hands. "I still don't get it . . . but then again, I guess I don't need to."

"Thanks a lot, Joe. I owe you one."

"Good night, Olivia. Get some sleep," he said. "See you tomorrow in the dining room, bright and early." Joe grinned. "Miss Chickadee Finch: A star is born . . ."

After Olivia locked and chained the hotel-room door, she set Throckmorton on a desk. His back rested against a wall, next to a coverless shoebox. The shoebox was stuffed with envelopes.

Olivia pulled up a chair, put her elbows on the leather desk blotter, and rested her chin in her hands.

"I can't believe that Annaliese would give away her sock monkey, even if Great-Grandmama had asked her to . . . I mean, fans give me gifts all the time, but still . . . I was watching her—and the boys—and I could tell that they didn't recognize me. . . ."

She pulled a pack of white envelopes out of the shoebox and removed the rubber band that held them together.

One by one, she shuffled through them.

"Judge Ellis W. Easterling, Eastcliff-by-the-Sea, Bay Fortune, Maine," she read. "Return to Sender."

"Evan Easterling. Return to Sender."

"Theodore Easterling. Return to Sender."

"Annaliese Easterling. Return to—"

Olivia dropped her chin and wept into her arms.

A few moments later, her facial expression changed from despair to anger. "I gave up," she said, slapping the desktop. "I should've kept fighting!"

Olivia rose to her feet and started pacing, from the bathroom to the dresser, from the door to the nightstand. Twice, she picked up the telephone receiver and slammed it back down.

"It's my fault . . . I shouldn't have listened to Great-Grandmama. There was no reason to wait. We should've done it my way—up front and honest."

Olivia covered the shoebox and tied it with twine. She laid two pieces of luggage out on the bed. One was a brown and ordinary suitcase. Into the second, a patent-leather hatbox, she placed Miss Chickadee Finch's black cap.

She penned a brief note on hotel stationary and sealed it inside a matching envelope. Using Throckmorton's yellow duck diaper pin, she secured the envelope to his chest.

Ouch!

"Sorry, little buddy," she apologized, as if she'd sensed his pain.

She pulled a dark gray cape off a hanger in the closet and slipped it over her shoulders. Then she picked up the phone. "Operator, please connect me with Room 117."

The telephone rang many times before someone on the other end of the line answered.

"Joe, I need to talk to you," Olivia said. "I'm coming to your room. Yes. Right now. Let me in."

Inside Joe's room, Olivia pulled a road map out of her handbag.

The bandleader, dressed in slacks and a half-buttoned shirt, rubbed the sleep out of his eyes. "Where do you think you're going?"

"By what time do we have to be in Cannon City?" Olivia asked.

"Setup and sound check's tomorrow, two p.m. sharp," Joe told her. "Why?"

Olivia glanced at her watch. "How many hours will it take to get there?"

"In this weather?" said Joe. "At least three."

"Then there's time."

"Time for what?"

Olivia explained that she wanted to borrow Joe's station wagon. She needed to return to the house where the party had been. If he refused, she'd bow out of the Cannon City engagement entirely and find another way back to Eastcliff.

"Olivia, you can't! Tonight's gig is no costume party. It's the Chesterfield Club," he reminded her. "Bright lights, big city, big money—and," he added, "the first night of Miss Chickadee Finch's North American Tour."

Bright lights in a big city . . . The Chesterfield Club . . . Oh, how glamorous and exciting that sounded.

Throckmorton almost wished that he could tag along.

"There's been some kind of mistake," Olivia argued. "The sock monkey is not mine. I have to take it back."

"Mail it," Joe said.

Olivia flashed two fingers in Joe's face. "Two hours—max—that's all the time I need to get there and back. It's still dark. Come on, Joe, cut me a break."

"I'm warning you, Miss Finch—you're under contract."

"In that case, I'd better get going."

"No, *we'd* better get going," Joe said, grabbing an overcoat and his car keys. "I have to make sure that you'll be back in time."

"Fine, but let me drive," said Olivia. "I know the way like the back of my hand."

Olivia followed Joe out the hotel's front door. The moon, full and round and bright, beamed down on the street where Joe's station wagon was parked.

"Once we're on the road," Joe said, "remind me to tell you what happened at that party after you left." His voice dropped off. "Strangest sight I ever saw . . ."

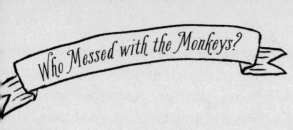

The steering wheel of Joe's automobile grazed Throckmorton's nose every time Olivia shifted gears. A heater fan blew warm air across his smiling face. Pinned to his chest, the envelope fluttered.

What words, he wondered, had Olivia written on the note inside?

Olivia kept her eyes focused on the road ahead. She appeared less distraught and more determined. Every so often she smiled and patted Throckmorton's leg. "Don't worry . . . I'm taking you home."

Throckmorton felt overjoyed to be heading back to Eastcliff, but mighty worried as well.

Just as Ebenezer had overheard Great-Grandmama say, Olivia couldn't walk back into her children's lives as if she'd never been gone. Was Olivia foolish enough to think that she could knock on Judge Easterling's door and he'd invite her back in?

After yawning more than a few times, Olivia pulled into the parking lot of an all-night diner. Joe had his thermos filled with coffee and they drove on. When they both had paper cups of hot coffee in hand, Olivia asked Joe what had happened at the party.

"After you left, the joint got jumping," said Joe. "Everyone was dancing and having a good time.

"All of a sudden the guy who lives there—some well-known judge, I heard—marches onto the stage in the middle of a number. He tells me to stop the music and grabs my mike."

"Why?" Olivia asked.

"In a nutshell, he announces that Great-Grandmama Easterling has been taken to the hospital and that the party is over. When someone asks what's wrong with her," Joe continued, "the judge says that it's too early to tell, that he'll know more in the morning.

"'If you're staying here,' he tells them, 'go back to your rooms; if you're not, the horses are harnessed and the sleighs are ready to take you down to your cars.'

"Some of the folks weren't too happy; they wanted to keep on dancing. But the judge wouldn't budge. He handed me a check and told the band to hit the road."

Joe took a few sips of coffee. "Then a few guys near the punch bowl started shouting out stuff like: 'Hey, what about Great-Grandmama's will? Did you talk her into leaving everything to you?'"

"And what did he say to that?" Olivia asked.

"It turns out that the old lady's cane was still leaning against that rose-colored chair. The judge grabbed the cane, leaped off the stage, and started swinging." Joe chuckled and slapped his knee. "That was the last I saw of those guys."

Although technically it wasn't funny, Throckmorton chuckled too. He couldn't wait to hear Sir Rudyard's version of this unfortunate event.

Now Joe was laughing so hard he had to stop and wipe the tears from his eyes. "So he's still swinging granny's cane, shouting, 'The party's over, I say!'—and he starts herding everyone out of the ballroom like they're a bunch of dumb sheep."

"Serves them right," said Olivia.

"Wait. It gets better," Joe said. "All of a sudden, I hear this blood-curdling scream. It's that woman with a wand in the purple cape. She's over by the wall screeching like a banshee."

At this point in his story, a hint of compassion crept into Joe's voice. "How do I put this?" He paused and took a deep breath of air. "Someone had messed with the monkeys."

"What do you mean—messed with the monkeys?"

"Tore off their costumes, slit their seams. Stuffing and little red hearts scattered all over the place."

Throckmorton's mind went blank. No words, no curses, no exclamations could adequately express his anguish.

"It was like a bad movie," Joe continued. "The *St. Valentine's Day Sock Monkey Massacre* . . ."

Olivia put her hands over her ears and screeched, "Stop!"

The car swerved and Joe lurched across the seat to steady the wheel.

"Who would do such a thing?" she wailed. "And why?"

"I figure that whoever did it," Joe said, "was looking for something. You know, like the prize inside a Cracker Jack box."

Throckmorton felt like his heart was being squeezed to death by a strong fist. He didn't know who would do such a thing, but he did know why.

Haunted by the image of his wounded comrades, he made a mental list of possible suspects: Evan, Teddy, their first cousins, second cousins, second-cousins-twice-removed, aunts, uncles . . . why, the list was endless . . . anyone could have heard the diamond-in-the-heart rumor and decided to find out if it was true.

"I can't believe it. . . ." Olivia sighed. "Or maybe I can."

Joe drained the last swallow of coffee out of his

cup. "Slow down. I think that's our turn, coming up on the right."

"And then . . . ," Joe continued.

"I don't know if I want to know," Olivia said.

"Bud—who'd hopped off the stage to take a closer look—started picking up the sock monkeys, and the judge went nuts! He told Bud to stand back—cease and desist!—that he was destroying the evidence.

"He started swinging that cane again. Bud and all the guests took off running, and he locked the doors behind them. 'I'll get to the bottom of this, if it's the last thing I do!' I heard him yell, while me and the rest of the band hightailed it out the back way."

"Holy macaroni," said Olivia. "What a mess . . ."

"Do you want to turn back?"

"No, Joe," she answered. "I've already come too far."

Follow the Leader

Olivia dimmed the headlights and down-shifted the gears. She braked Joe's automobile near a stand of tall pines on the snowy lane that led to Eastcliff.

She pulled on the tight gray gloves that she'd worn onstage the night before and then stepped out of the car with Throckmorton tucked under her arm.

"I'll walk the rest of the way, Joe. I want Donald to see that it's me and not a stranger, so he won't bark."

"Who's Donald?" asked Joe.

"A very large dog."

Joe moved into the driver's seat. His eyes narrowed. "You've been here before—before last night, I mean."

She laid her hand on Joe's shoulder. "Someday," she promised, "I'll tell you the whole story."

"I'll wait in the car," Joe said. "You've got twenty minutes—max—or I'm coming in after you."

Olivia and Throckmorton made their way up the lane. A few red velvet hearts still clung to snow-covered boughs hanging low to the ground, but most had fallen. Soon, Throckmorton thought, their color would start to bleed.

Up ahead, Eastcliff's windows were dark and shuttered, except for the one in the kitchen, yellowed with light. Tire tracks dented the newly fallen snow.

Maybe the judge and Annaliese's brothers had already departed for the train that would take Evan and Teddy to boarding school.

Throckmorton certainly hoped so. Eastcliff had many rooms, but he didn't believe that a single one had space enough for forgiveness.

Right then Donald emerged from his dog house. He raised his snout high in the air, sniffed the wind, and wagged a happy tail. Olivia tramped through the snow, untethered the chain, and set him free.

Mrs. Wiggins's head appeared in the kitchen window.

Smiling, Olivia waved Throckmorton above her head like a flag of truce.

Mrs. Wiggins scuttled out the door. Her eyes widened. Her hands rushed to cover her mouth.

After a moment, she motioned Olivia, Throckmorton, and Donald forward.

Inside Eastcliff's kitchen, Throckmorton inhaled the delicious scents of home: cinnamon, scalded milk, yeast, and sweet dough rising.

Quickly, Olivia explained why she'd come and

begged Mrs. Wiggins to let her pass. "I'll go up the servants' staircase. No one will see me. I won't wake her, I promise." She glanced at her watch. "I won't have time."

Mrs. Wiggins suspiciously eyed the envelope pinned to Throckmorton's chest. "I can see that Annaliese gets her sock monkey back."

"No offense, Mrs. Wiggins, but I don't trust anyone around here."

"I—I just don't know . . . ," the flustered cook argued. "I mean . . ."

Olivia's voice was the voice of a woman on Death Row pleading for mercy. "Please."

"Breakfast is in the dining room at nine. The hired help will be coming down soon to help me make the meal. So go on then, but make it snappy." The cook dipped her fingers into her apron pocket. "If you get caught, don't blame me. I'll swear that I never saw you."

"I won't get caught," Olivia said.

"If you're quiet, Annaliese shouldn't wake up. Last night was quite a night . . . but I guess you already knew that."

Olivia gave her a quizzical look.

"I knew it was you from the first note you sang."

"You remembered," said Olivia, with a slight smile of satisfaction. "Did anyone else? I thought one of the boys might recognize my voice. I used to sing to the children, you know . . ."

"Put a move on it," said Mrs. Wiggins, "before your ex-in-laws wake up and start stirring up trouble. And don't worry about bumping into the judge or the boys. They're not here . . . but that's another story."

"I've missed you," said Olivia sadly, squeezing Mrs. Wiggins's hand. "By the way, which room is hers?"

"She's still in the nursery."

Olivia raised her eyebrows.

"She's got a bigger bed. One of her nannies, I forget which one, painted it pink. Everything else is pretty much the same as you left it."

"Hold on to Donald, will you?" Olivia asked. "This time when I go, maybe I can take him with me."

"Oh, no you don't! Donald is my dog now," Mrs. Wiggins retorted, wagging her finger. "And don't even *think* about taking anyone else," she warned.

A few steps from the nursery, Olivia paused. Annaliese's bedroom door was cracked open. Every other door on the second floor was closed. Cautiously, she poked her head around the open door. "Her bed's empty," she whispered.

Empty? But why? Throckmorton wondered.

Where is she? What happened?

Rattled, Throckmorton's imagination ran wild . . .

Maybe Annaliese discovered her mistake, ran outside, and tried catch up with Joe's car. Maybe she got lost. Maybe she's out there somewhere, cold and buried in snow.

Olivia stepped cautiously into Annaliese's bedroom. Throckmorton fully expected that she'd set him down on the bed and go while the going was good.

Instead, a small piece of paper lying on the nightstand caught Olivia's attention. She stuck her gloves into her handbag and picked up the handwritten note.

She read quietly:

Dear Annaliese,

By the time you read this, Evan and I will be on the train heading to our new school. I wish that you could have come with us.

Evan told me to tell you that he's sorry he blabbed your secret about the diamond inside Ebenezer's heart. He never thought that something so awful would happen.

And just so you know, I didn't tell him anything else. I swear!

Hey, could you do me a favor? Father locked the ballroom doors, but you know how to get in. Will you find Captain Eugene and *try to fix him up for me? Hide him until I get back, okay?*

Your brother,

Teddy

P. S. Fix up Sir Rudyard, too, Evan says.

"Now what?" Olivia asked herself.

At that moment, Bailey wandered in. The sleuth hound shuffled up and sniffed Olivia's feet. He straightened his tail, turned around, and trotted off like a scout on a very important mission.

When Olivia didn't follow, Bailey yelped. He threw back his head as if to say, *Hurry up! What are you waiting for?*

Throckmorton prayed that Olivia would play it safe. Great-Grandmama's cautionary words echoed in his mind:

This isn't the time . . . this isn't the place . . .

(Throckmorton couldn't have agreed more.)

Why oh why, after all this time, he wordlessly challenged her, *would you place your fate in the paws of a dog?*

Olivia didn't hear him, of course.

And even if she had, Throckmorton was pretty sure that Annaliese's mother wouldn't have listened.

Olivia clutched Throckmorton face-forward in her clammy hands and trailed Bailey up the servants' staircase to the rear entrance to the ballroom.

The back door was wide open.

At the threshold she froze. She drew her breath in sharply.

Annaliese sat cross-legged and alone on the ballroom floor. Drawn and pale, she held a needle and thread in her hand. A sock monkey without a costume lay across her lap.

Wearing her favorite nightgown, Annaliese looked like a little blue boat of hope floating in a sea strewn with injured sock monkeys.

Wreckage was everywhere: puffs of discarded stuffing; red felt hearts, flat and empty; pieces of cast-off costumes; arms, arms, and more arms.

Curses, curses, infinite curses on the rogue who perpetrated this crime!

Throckmorton raged at the injustice.

And yet, a strange sensation swept over him at the same time. Instead of feeling relieved that he'd been spared, he felt guilty that he'd survived.

From this distance, it appeared that the phony sock monkeys, still heaped in a pile, hadn't been messed with: proof that the thief had known exactly what he or she was looking for.

Olivia released a deep breath. She took one step forward. Her hands trembled.

Suddenly, from the opposite side of the ballroom, Throckmorton heard the loud snap of a lock.

The double doors swung open.

Olivia quickly slipped back into the shadows.

"Annaliese," Miss Pine exclaimed, rushing to her side. "What are you doing in here? I've been looking all over for you! It's practically the middle of the night. You're supposed to be in bed."

Tears welled up in Annaliese's eyes. "It's *my* fault!" she shrieked. "I *have* to fix them!"

"That can't be true," said Miss Pine, crouching down beside her. "What do you mean?"

"I broke my promise! I told Teddy about the diamond and he told Evan and Evan told . . ."

Miss Pine grasped Annaliese's arm. The needle and thread dropped from her hand. The injured sock monkey tumbled out of her lap.

"What promise? What diamond?"

Now Annaliese was crying so hard that she almost couldn't speak. "I—I didn't . . .

"Keep . . .

"The secret . . . and . . .

"Now the sock monkeys are ruined . . .

"And no one's going to want them back!"

Miss Pine gripped Annaliese's shoulders. She looked squarely into her eyes. "Annaliese, you didn't harm the monkeys. It's not your fault—you have to believe me."

Miss Pine pulled Annaliese close to her chest. Olivia's long fingernails dug deeper and deeper into Throckmorton's skin, the pain like an arrow piercing his heart.

"I was bad," Annaliese blubbered. "I was a bad baby, too—Madge told me so—and that's why my mother went away. And now she's gone and I missed my chance and I gave that Joe guy the wrong monkey and I'll never see her or Throckmorton ever again."

"No! That's not true!" Olivia cried out suddenly. "Madge lied! You weren't a bad baby! That's not why I left!"

Annaliese's fingers flew to the locket that hung around her neck.

"Throckmorton!" she screamed, scrambling to her feet. "And YOU!"

What a remarkable moment . . .

Throckmorton was home at last, blissfully squished inside Olivia and Annaliese's embrace.

Mother's and daughter's tears mingled and

sprinkled on his pretzel-shaped ears, more tiny medals of honor he'd treasure for the rest of his life.

Miss Pine, who'd stepped back to give Olivia and Annaliese room, came forward, offering Olivia her hand. "Miss Pine," she said warmly. "Miss Laurel Pine. Welcome."

The smiling nanny tousled Annaliese's hair. "And I've got some other good news. That wicked Madge is gone and she's never coming back."

"She isn't?"

"Madge packed up and left sometime last night. She told Mrs. Wiggins that she was sick and tired of working for the Easterlings."

Good riddance!

Annaliese shifted Throckmorton's body so that his chin rested on her shoulder. "Wait a minute," she said, noticing the note pinned to his chest. "What's this?"

"You can read it later," Olivia whispered.

At that very moment, Throckmorton spied a silent and imposing figure filling the doorframe that Miss Pine had just passed through.

Jumping jackrabbits!

It was Judge Easterling!

How long had *he* been standing there?

Annaliese wiped her nose with her sleeve. "But the sock monkeys," she sniffed, "I have to fix them—

before everyone wakes up. Before Father gets home."

Now, like an actor who'd just been given his cue to come onstage, the judge quietly approached Annaliese.

The judge's eyes met Olivia's. He stopped short. His mustache twitched like it had never twitched before.

"I *am* home," he announced.

Annaliese spun around. "Father, look! My mother is here."

Mother.

The word hung in the air like a bird trapped in the eye of a storm—the word that the children weren't allowed to say, yet one which was always hovering, wanting to land.

"Yes, Mrs. Wiggins warned me," he responded.

"Mother is Miss Chickadee Finch, the singer," Annaliese said excitedly. "I didn't recognize her. No one did!"

"Indeed." The judge nodded. "A clever disguise. Just as I suspected; Great-Grandmama Easterling had a trick up her sleeve."

"There's been some kind of mistake," Olivia tried to explain. "Annaliese gave Joe—the bandleader— her sock monkey to give to me. I didn't know why."

"You're the one who made the mistake," he snarled.

Olivia's face turned ashen. "I know that I'm not welcome here . . . forbidden, actually, from ever coming back . . ."

Annaliese held her father in her gaze. "Father, you wouldn't let Mother come back?"

Throckmorton fully expected the judge to deny it. Plead the Fifth Amendment or some such thing.

The judge fell silent.

"That's not fair," Annaliese told the man who spent his days sitting in judgment of others. "Why, all these years, I've been waiting and wondering and . . ."

Annaliese turned her back on him.

With Throckmorton tucked safely under her left arm, she marched to where Ebenezer the Lighthouse Keeper was sitting.

She picked up the sock monkey—that she'd sewn by hand and stitched with love—and put it into Olivia's outstretched hands.

"This is Ebenezer," Annaliese told her. "He's a lighthouse keeper. He's the monkey meant for you, not Throckmorton." Annaliese cocked her head. "How did you know that I'd made a mistake?"

"I didn't," Olivia answered. "I thought Throckmorton was some kind of sign, a sign that you wanted me to come back."

"I've always wanted you to come back."

The room went silent. Olivia's chin dropped

to her chest. After a few moments, she turned Ebenezer's brown-and-cream body up, down, and all around. "They're almost exactly the same size," she observed. "And they've got the same ears. It would be easy to get them mixed up."

"I made Ebenezer," Annaliese said. "Great-Grandmama taught me how."

The judge heaved an exasperated sigh.

"Perhaps I'd better go now," Olivia said. "I didn't come here to cause trouble. I have a car waiting."

"No!" Annaliese said firmly. "You're not leaving! Nobody's leaving. Not until the sock monkeys are fixed."

The judge protested, "But—but—she . . ."

"Shush!" Annaliese scolded. "You're upsetting them! They've been hurt—badly!—and we have to put them back together."

Miss Pine, who'd been quietly gathering sock monkeys in her arms, nodded in agreement.

Annaliese's eyes bore into her mother first and then her father.

"Your fight can wait."

"What do you want me to do?" Olivia asked, slipping off her hooded cape.

Olivia didn't have time to help, Throckmorton realized. She had less than twenty minutes. Joe was waiting outside.

"Breakfast's at nine," said Miss Pine, checking her watch. "Folks will start waking up around eight. That gives us less than two hours."

Annaliese cupped her hand over her chin. "Hmm . . . let me think."

After a few moments, her eyes lit up. "I've got an idea."

"Father, you line the sock monkeys up in their chairs along the wall, smallest to largest. Then match their arms with their bodies the best you can. Luckily, only their left arms were snipped off."

"Miss Pine, pick up the hearts and pile them right there." Annaliese pointed toward the spot on the floor next to where she'd been sewing. "Then gather up the stuffing and put a few handfuls inside each monkey."

"I will," said Miss Pine, "gladly."

"And since you're so good with costumes, Mother," Annaliese said with a smile, "you can piece their outfits together and dress them back up."

She held up Great-Grandmama's ledger and a pen that Great-Uncle George had left behind. "This will make your job easier."

"I'll give each sock monkey a heart and stitch their arms back on, the way Great-Grandmama taught me."

"Good thinking," said Miss Pine as she and

the judge set out to do their jobs. "A sock monkey reassembly line."

Annaliese and Olivia set Throckmorton and Ebenezer against the sewing basket, and then Annaliese sat down. Olivia remained close by, filling her hands with random bits and pieces of the sock monkey costumes: a little leather shoe, a fez hat, pom-poms, a string of pearls, Sir Rudyard's suspenders.

"I wish I knew which heart belonged to which monkey," Annaliese told Olivia. "But I guess it doesn't matter. Great-Grandmama used the same cookie cutter to make them all." Her voice dropped to a whisper. "Only Ebenezer's heart is different."

A puzzled look crossed Olivia's face. "Why's that?"

Annaliese pressed her pointer finger over her lips. "There's a huge diamond inside his heart. I put it there myself. Great-Grandmama wanted you to have it."

"How can that be?" Olivia asked quietly.

Annaliese picked up the sewing scissors. "If you want to see it . . . ," she offered, albeit reluctantly. "I guess I can always sew Ebenezer back together . . ."

"No. I'm not going to do that," Olivia said. "Not now. Not ever. I've broken enough hearts in my life."

Mended Hearts

Later, Throckmorton would learn that Mrs. Wiggins had done everything in her power to prevent Joe from coming after Olivia.

When Joe knocked on Eastcliff's kitchen door demanding to see his band's soloist, the morning buns that the cook had made—rich and twisted with cinnamon and sugar—were hot out of the oven. She brewed a fresh pot of coffee, tempting Joe with a promise to tell him a few things about Olivia that he might not know. She located a map and showed him a shortcut to Cannon City.

The original limit—twenty minutes—turned into an hour or more.

By the time Joe and Mrs. Wiggins and Donald came into the ballroom, thirty-nine smiling sock monkeys sat in thirty-nine sock-monkey-sized chairs along the ballroom wall.

Only one red-heeled sock monkey remained in need of repair: Miss Beatrice. Already frayed and frail, the judge's sock monkey had suffered greatly at the hands of the thief.

The judge and Olivia hovered above their daughter as she examined Miss Beatrice's wounds.

The cook, bandleader, bloodhound, and Great Dane formed a respectful half circle around them.

"Father, my hands are tired," Annaliese said. "I could use some help."

"What do you want me to do?" he asked, bending low.

"Put Miss Beatrice's heart back where it belongs." She handed him her needle and thread. "Then sew her arm back on."

"All the red felt hearts are gone," the judge told her. "Laurel—I mean, Miss Pine—and I've looked everywhere. We can't find any more."

Lost in thought, Annaliese ran her fingers back and forth across the locket's gold chain. Unexpectedly, she undid the clasp. She dangled the necklace in front of her father.

"Miss Beatrice should have a special heart."

The judge was caught off guard. "Well, um . . . uh, I don't really know if . . ."

Annaliese pressed the precious locket into his hand. "I know that it would make her happy."

"But . . . but, maybe . . ."

Not yet swayed, the judge searched Miss Pine's face, hoping, no doubt, that she'd come up with a better solution. "After all, I think—"

"It's a wonderful idea!" Miss Pine interjected.

Mrs. Wiggins was more than happy to put in her

two cents. "Sometimes it's best to bury the past, I always say."

"The locket's mine," said Olivia. "And I can't imagine a better place for it."

The judge could see that the odds were stacked against him. "A fine idea," he said with as much enthusiasm as he could muster.

He gently wriggled the locket into place. "Like this?" he asked Annaliese.

"Yup." The dimples deepened in her cheeks. "She'll need a little more stuffing. Fill up the empty spaces . . . yes, that's right."

"And then?" he asked.

Annaliese handed him a few straight pins. "Then reattach her arm and stitch the seam."

The threads at the top of Miss Beatrice's left arm were ragged; Judge Easterling's stitching was clumsy and painfully slow.

When he finally finished, Olivia handed him Miss Beatrice's Scottish-style outfit. "Unless I made a mistake, this belongs to her."

"If no one minds," the judge said, "I think I'd like Miss Beatrice to go back to being the way she was when Great-Grandmama made her. She didn't come with any kind of costume at all."

"She didn't?" asked Annaliese.

"No. And I never knew why. In those days, all the

others did. When my cousins asked her name, I lied and told them that my sock monkey was a boy—a boy named Bear."

Miss Pine put her hand over her mouth to stifle a smile.

Throckmorton smiled too.

Throckmorton and Miss Beatrice . . . a natural pair.

From the floor below came the sounds of houseguests stirring. Olivia checked the time on her watch. "Oh my gosh! We'd better hit the road."

"Darn right," said Joe.

"Where are you going?" Annaliese asked.

"To Cannon City," Olivia answered. "I'm singing with the band tonight."

Annaliese's eyes brightened. "May I come along?" she asked eagerly.

"If you want to . . . I mean, I'd like you to, but you'd have to ask your father."

Annaliese pulled Throckmorton into her arms as if he might bring her luck. "May I, Father?" she asked.

Throckmorton knew the answer before the judge got it out of his mouth. Even a sock monkey could understand how wary and suspicious Annaliese's father must be.

The judge shook his head. "No."

"Please, Ellis," Olivia said. "Annaliese wants to go. And I want her to come. I haven't seen her in almost nine years. It's only one night. We'll drive up today and I'll bring her back tomorrow. Twenty-four hours, that's all I'm asking."

"I—I can't allow . . . ," he protested. "Surely you can't be serious."

Annaliese's face fell.

One tiny, errant teardrop pinned itself on Throckmorton's chest.

"You don't trust me," Olivia said. "I understand. But I promise . . ."

"Your promises aren't worth much, Olivia," the judge responded tersely.

Annaliese rose to her feet. "Father, do you mean that I can't go with Mother *now*?" she asked. "Or that I can't go with Mother *ever*?"

What could the judge say? What could he do?

Not only was his daughter a formidable presence, but she was backed by a battalion of red-heeled sock monkeys armed with the power to soften his heart.

The poor man didn't stand a chance.

The judge hemmed.

He hawed.

And finally answered: "Not today."

Not today? It took Throckmorton a few

moments to figure out what the judge meant.

Hurrah! Huzzah!

"Not today" was the judge's way of saying "someday."

Someday the judge *would* let Annaliese go with her mother.

"I promised Great-Grandmama," he told Olivia, "that I'd bring Annaliese to the hospital this afternoon."

"Great-Grandmama!" Annaliese blurted. "I forgot to ask . . . Did you see her? Is she going to be all right?"

"Hopefully," the judge replied. "She's had a stroke. Mild, but still, at her age . . ."

"I understand about today," Olivia said. "But I also heard you say that Annaliese may come with me another time."

"Yes, that's what I said."

Miss Pine, Mrs. Wiggins, and Joe exchanged looks of happy surprise.

Annaliese marched to the sidelines. She plucked Sir Rudyard and Captain Eugene out of their chairs and brought them into the fold.

"And what about Evan and Teddy?" she asked her father. "They couldn't go today either, of course, but may they also go see Mother someday?"

"Yes." Judge Easterling had an odd look on his

face—a mixture of defeat, sadness, and perhaps relief.

"You have my word."

Now the lineup of sock monkeys smiled their broadest smiles and cheered their loudest cheers. "Hip-hip-hooray! Not today, but someday!"

None of the humans heard their cheers, but Donald and Bailey perked their ears and howled joyfully.

Joe stepped forward. "I don't care who comes— today or next week or next year," he barked, "as long as we leave NOW."

"I'll walk Mother out," Annaliese told her father, swinging Throckmorton by the tail.

Miss Pine lightly touched the judge's arm.

"Life's not always fair," she said softly. "But sometimes, it can be fixed."

F or a few precious moments, Annaliese and Olivia were alone. They perched side by side, like two birds of the same species, on the bottom step of the servants' staircase. Throckmorton and Ebenezer sat happily in their laps.

Before leaving the ballroom, Annaliese had ripped a square of paper off the crushed *Starring Miss Chickadee Finch* stage sign. On it she printed five words in large letters—*FREE TO A FOREVER HOME*—and mounted her handmade sign on top of the pile of phony sock monkeys.

Throckmorton was proud of Annaliese for doing so. Most everybody, he decided, deserved a second chance.

Olivia had asked Joe to go outside and warm up the car while she and Annaliese said good-bye. He willingly complied. Throckmorton was beginning to think that the flashy leader of the Bird Land Big Band had a crush on his soon-to-be-famous soloist.

"You don't look like your photograph," Annaliese said, the first one to speak.

"No, I don't," Olivia replied. "It was taken a long time ago."

"Now you look like . . ."

Olivia ran her fingers through her close-cropped hair. "Yes, I know. A bird."

"Miss Chickadee Finch," said Annaliese. "It's a silly name. But I like it."

"It's all part of the act," Olivia said, patting Annaliese's knee. "It was Joe's idea." She smiled. "I tried Miss Scarlet Tanager and Miss Robin Redbreast, but they didn't stick."

"Mrs. Ellis Easterling, too," Annaliese matter-of-factly reminded her.

"You must be very angry with me."

Annaliese scrunched up her face and shoulders. "It's hard to be mad at someone you've never known."

Olivia's face burned a deep shade of red. "I couldn't come back, Annaliese. I didn't know how."

"But you're here now."

"Yes." Olivia nodded. "Your great-grandmother helped me find a way."

"Why did you leave?" Annaliese asked. "I don't understand . . . no one would tell me."

"Someday, when there's time, I'll tell you the whole story," Olivia promised. "But here's the short version: Ellis was traveling around Europe. We met in Hamburg, where I was singing in a café. I was young and foolish. We eloped.

"Then we moved here, to Eastcliff. I thought I

loved him, and then I thought I didn't—and I was afraid I never would. I needed some time to think.

"My brother, Karl, had come to the States looking for me. Your father didn't believe that Karl was my brother. He got angry. He told me I was a bad mother and not to bother coming back." Olivia clenched her fists. "I should have fought harder. I was a coward. I gave up."

Here, she broke down and started to cry.

"I was so sad and so depressed and so . . . ashamed."

Olivia could barely get the words out.

"I couldn't forgive myself for what I'd done—to Ellis, to the boys, to you. The longer I stayed away, the harder it was to come back."

Annaliese squeezed her mother's hand. "But not anymore."

"No. Not anymore."

Annaliese leaned her head against Olivia's shoulder. "I've already forgiven you, you know."

"You have?"

"Just like Throckmorton did when I left him in the net," Annaliese told her. "Forgiving is not always as hard as it seems."

The loud, insistent honking of an automobile's horn interrupted whatever Olivia might have wanted to say.

She plucked a folded piece of paper out of her handbag and pressed it into Annaliese's palm. "This is my schedule—the dates, cities, and names of all the clubs where I'll be performing over the next couple of months."

"Wow."

"Hang on to it," Olivia told her. "Then you'll always know where I am. And if you ever need to reach me, tell Miss Pine—she'll know how to track me down." She smiled sadly. "It looks to me like your nanny's going to be around for a long time—if you get what I mean."

"Miss Pine's okay, but she's not as good as a *real* mother."

Olivia and Annaliese stood up. Olivia drew Annaliese into her arms. This time both Throckmorton and Ebenezer got crushed in their scrumptious hug.

"But Miss Pine is right about one thing, young lady," Olivia said, wagging her finger. "You should be in bed."

After Olivia, Ebenezer, and Joe drove away, Annaliese first returned to the ballroom, where she helped Judge Easterling and Miss Pine make arrangements to return the repaired sock monkeys to their keepers.

Only after that was accomplished did she and Throckmorton go back to bed.

Throckmorton would learn later that every single sock monkey went back to their rightful homes again. And all of the phony sock monkeys were adopted.

Neither Judge Easterling, nor any of his relatives, ever told Great-Grandmama what happened on the night of her ninetieth-birthday party. Humbled by the sight of their wounded sock monkeys, Ethel Constance Easterling's descendants kept it a closely guarded family secret.

Spring came early to Eastcliff-by-the-Sea that

year. Balmy March winds blew, the frozen sea cracked open, and purple crocuses pushed through melting snow.

In early April, Judge Easterling announced his intention to court Miss Pine in the old-fashioned way. Annaliese's former nanny moved into the carriage house to help Great-Grandmama recuperate, and Annaliese enrolled in the local school.

Every day a picture postcard arrived, each one sent by Olivia from a different city on the East Coast. Annaliese pinned each postcard on a bulletin board next to her bed. Pinned between a postcard from Boston and another from Baltimore was the note that Olivia had written to Annaliese on hotel stationary. Throckmorton had heard Annaliese read it aloud so often that he had the eight words memorized:

I love you.

I'm sorry.

Please forgive me.

Throckmorton also found out that once, when Olivia was performing in a town nearby, she took a day off from her tour to visit Evan and Teddy at St. John's Military Academy. At first, Evan had a hard time agreeing to give his mother a second chance, but Teddy readily forgave her.

Throckmorton, Captain Eugene, Sir Rudyard,

and Miss Beatrice spent countless happy hours at the tiny lace-covered table in the corner of Annaliese's room. As a result of many deep, philosophical, and insightful discussions, they agreed that sock monkeys and keepers alike heal at different times in different ways. And that a secret is safest when everyone knows it.

One day, the topic of the sock monkey massacre came up—a sore subject, to be sure. Boldly, Throckmorton asked the question that he'd been dying to ask: "Who did it?"

"No one knows," said Sir Rudyard. "He, or she, was in disguise."

"A black mask," Captain Eugene said.

"Black wig," Miss Beatrice recalled.

"Black floppy hat," said Sir Rudyard. "Putrid breath and . . ."

All three sock monkeys chanted at the same time: "Hands. That. Smelled. Like. Fish."

Hands that smelled like fish?

Bingo!

"Madge!" Throckmorton shouted.

"That lazy maid?" asked Captain Eugene, incredulous.

Yes, that lazy maid, who soon thereafter was arrested. Police found her with a pocketful of precious jewels that pirates had once stolen from a Spanish king. Not surprisingly, the authorities uncovered a substantial stash of objects pilfered from Eastcliff-by-the-Sea. Subsequently, the crown jewels were returned to Spain's royal family, and the family's heirlooms to the Easterling estate.

As far as Throckmorton was concerned, *The Story of a Lazy Maid Named Madge* ended happily ever after.

She was thrown in the slammer and never seen nor heard from again.

Hooray!

Finally—finally!—Annaliese's promised "some-day" arrived.

A few months after Great-Grandmama's ninetieth-birthday party ball, Olivia and Ebenezer the Lighthouse Keeper and Annaliese and Throckmorton met up in Cannon City, where they entered the glamorous lobby of the Chesterfield Club.

In their earlier appearance in February, the Bird Land Big Band, starring Miss Chickadee Finch, had brought the crowd to their feet: a standing ovation. The club's manager straightaway booked the band for a return engagement.

Annaliese was almost ten years old now and looking very grown-up. She wore a plum-and-blue paisley dress with a dropped waist, raglan sleeves, and lace cuffs, and a new pair of stacked-heel shoes. Her long hair was brushed into soft waves.

She'd dressed Throckmorton in a bright blue V-neck sweater. Knitted by Miss Pine, the sweater covered his yellow duck diaper pin ever-so-nicely. A striped hand-knit wool scarf was wrapped loosely around his neck. When Annaliese held him up to

Olivia's engraved hand mirror, Throckmorton liked what he saw.

Très chic! A look of casual sophistication that suited him quite well.

As their party of four—Annaliese, Olivia, Throckmorton, and Ebenezer—approached the host stand at the club, the maître d' glanced up, down, and all around.

The maître d's eyes seemed to be asking: *Is this some kind of a joke?*

The expression on his face read:

Sock monkeys?

At the Chesterfield Club?

Impossible!

He quickly regained his composure and extended his hand for a shake. "Good evening, Miss Finch. Welcome back to the Chesterfield Club. It's a pleasure to see you again."

"I'd like a table for four please, for me and my friends," Olivia said, but then corrected herself. "I mean, for me and my family."

The maître d' checked his seating chart. "I just happen to have . . . the best seats in the house available."

Holy Hollywood!

The best seats in the house!

Sizzling bolts of excitement zigzagged up, down,

and across Throckmorton's tail. He could get used to this kind of life pretty quickly.

"And we'll need a couple of pillows, or something," Olivia added. "You know—for the monkeys."

"Of course, Miss Finch." The maître d' bowed. "I'll let your waiter know."

Later, after every song that Olivia sang, the audience broke into wild applause. Many of her fans had heard Miss Chickadee Finch sing before, but they'd never heard her sing the way she sang that night.

Before the last song of her final set, Olivia invited Annaliese and Throckmorton to join her onstage. A stage manager set a stool in the center of the stage for Annaliese to sit on.

A golden glow from a circle of footlights enveloped them. A spotlight from above momentarily blinded Throckmorton. Although the rest of the faces in the audience seemed blurred, Ebenezer's smile beamed ever-so-brightly.

Throckmorton might never know for sure whether or not he had a precious jewel hidden inside his own heart. It didn't matter. Right now, his body felt as if it were stuffed with stars.

"I'd like you to meet my daughter, Annaliese, and her sock monkey, Throckmorton," Olivia told her adoring fans.

She touched the top of his head gently, like a blessing. "Annaliese's great-grandmother, Ethel, made Throckmorton by hand. She gave him to Annaliese on the day she was born."

Olivia did her best to choke back her tears.

"If it hadn't been for Throckmorton," she said, "Annaliese wouldn't be here with me tonight."

She put her arm around Annaliese and drew her close.

"Please give them both a big hand."

It was Throckmorton's first taste of fame, and he loved it. He loved being onstage with everyone watching. He loved the sound of applause meant only for him. He loved the song that Olivia sang for his (pretzel-shaped) ears only as they waltzed around the stage:

Throck-monkey, Throck-monkey . . .

A most remarkable sock monkey . . .

For the rest of their long and happy lives, Annaliese never forgot about Throckmorton again.

Whenever the story of Ethel Constance Easterling's ninetieth-birthday party ball was told, Annaliese repeated Olivia's words—*If it hadn't been for Throckmorton*—like the refrain of a much-loved song.

Indeed, Mr. Throckmorton S. Monkey had achieved the impossible.

How? his sock monkey descendants would ask.
Simply by being himself:
Loving.
And loyal.
A very good listener.
And he never—not even once!—stopped smiling.

Acknowledgments

I'd like to shine the spotlight on six persons of "the human persuasion" who helped make my story about an irrepressible sock monkey named Throckmorton and Annaliese, the young girl whom he loved, the best book that it could be. I am deeply indebted to: Andrea Welch, my insightful and delightful editor, for her gentle yet challenging editorial guidance; Linda Pratt, my amazing agent, for believing in me as a writer and steadfastly promoting my work; Sarah Jane Wright, for bringing both whimsy and emotion to the characters through her charming illustrations; Lauren Rille, for her artistic vision and engaging book design; Donna Studer, a dear friend, for her unwavering enthusiasm and astute editorial assistance; and my kind and generous husband, Ralph, for his stalwart support, be it moral, editorial, technical, or culinary.

Now that *The Secrets of Eastcliff-by-the-Sea* is finally out in the world, I also see in my mind the smiling faces of innumerable writing colleagues and friends in the Twin Cities book community who have encouraged me along the way. Thanks to all of you who have listened to a chapter, cheered me on, read a draft, provided invaluable feedback, and gifted me with an entire cast of sock monkeys to keep me company while I wrote.

And, of course, extra special thanks to my family: Erin, Martin, Tadhg, Naoise, Jonathan, Lynn, Walden, Albert, Britt, Marcus, Janine, and Zaak, as well my canine companions, Daisy and Tango. Thank you for simply being yourselves—loving and loyal, very good listeners—and for enriching my life with your never-ending smiles.